Only, w...
there wa...
in her ex...
oh, yes!—...kisses.

Without allowing himself to consider how reckless it might be, he pulled her into his arms again. Closer this time. Reveled in the feel of her warm, curvaceous body against him as he lowered his head and kissed her again. Longer than the others. Much hotter, even as his hands began to roam against her, touching her back and below.

Enjoying the sound of her soft moan against his mouth.

His mind darted to the possibilities. The couch was too small a location for real enjoyment, but his bedroom wasn't far away in this tiny apartment.

But before he could lead her there, or even make the suggestion, she pulled away.

Dear Reader,

Canine Refuge is the fifth book in my Shelter of Secrets series for Harlequin Romantic Suspense, and as with the others in this series, it takes place primarily at the very special Chance Animal Shelter.

In this book, veterinary technician Janna Welles works at both the downtown Chance Animal Clinic and the clinic at the Chance Animal Shelter, a place that takes in both animals needing new homes and people in danger who need protection. She's surprised one day when a dog under her care bolts away despite his limp—and is stopped by a man walking in a hallway. Janna thinks she recognizes the man—yet surely that's not famous, bestselling author Nolan Hoffsler. But, yes, it is Nolan, whose life has been threatened after the publication of his most recent novel, which is based on a true story about a murder. Now someone is apparently after him to shut him up and get revenge. Janna is also an aspiring writer, and she gets to know Nolan, who's given the new identity of Josh Forlett after he's accepted at the shelter. He offers to critique her writing—and their attraction grows. But the threats against his life continue and Nolan believes he needs to leave. Janna wants him to remain safe and maybe in her life—and not only as a critiquer. Can both Nolan and their new relationship survive?

I hope you enjoy *Canine Refuge*. Please come visit me at my website, www.lindaojohnston.com, and at my weekly blog, killerhobbies.blogspot.com. And, yes, I'm on Facebook and Writerspace, too.

Linda O. Johnston

CANINE REFUGE

LINDA O. JOHNSTON

Harlequin

ROMANTIC SUSPENSE

ROMANTIC SUSPENSE™

ISBN-13: 978-1-335-50276-6

Canine Refuge

For questions and comments about the quality of this book, please contact us at CustomerService@Harlequin.com.

TM and ® are trademarks of Harlequin Enterprises ULC.

Harlequin Enterprises ULC
22 Adelaide St. West, 41st Floor
Toronto, Ontario M5H 4E3, Canada
www.Harlequin.com

Printed in Lithuania

Recycling programs for this product may not exist in your area.

MIX
Paper | Supporting responsible forestry
FSC® C021394

Linda O. Johnston loves to write. While honing her writing skills, she worked in advertising and public relations, then became a lawyer...and enjoyed writing contracts. Linda's first published fiction appeared in *Ellery Queen's Mystery Magazine* and won a Robert L. Fish Memorial Award for Best First Mystery Short Story of the Year. Linda now spends most of her time creating memorable tales of romantic suspense, paranormal romance and mystery. Visit www.lindaojohnston.com.

No surprise, like the other books in the
Shelter of Secrets series, *Canine Refuge* is
dedicated to the wonderful people who
devote their lives to helping other people in trouble,
and also to those who work for and volunteer at
shelters where dogs, cats and other animals without
human families are cared for. This time, I want to add
my fellow writers, who derive ideas from any source
that works—even if it might be dangerous!

And also, as I always do, I dedicate this book
to my dear husband, Fred, as well as our delightful,
loving dogs, Cari and Roxie.

Acknowledgments

This may be getting old, but I definitely mean it!
Yet again, many thanks to my amazing editor,
Allison Lyons, and my fantastic agent, Paige Wheeler.

Chapter 1

Janna Welles dashed out of the veterinary clinic and into the hallway of the Chance Animal Shelter's main building. Dressed in her usual blue scrubs, she was chasing Squeegee, one of the dogs under the clinic's care. Under *her* care for now, since she was the only veterinary technician on duty. Hard to tell that the chocolate Labrador retriever mix had a bad leg the way he ran down the hall, although he was limping a bit. Janna thought she had fully closed the door—but apparently not.

"Here, Squeegee," she called. "Squeegee, sit!"

A couple of men walking down the hall were now just in front of Squeegee. They both turned, and the guy on the right knelt and caught the dog in his arms.

One of the men was Scott Sherridan, the director of the Chance Animal Shelter, but the one who caught Squeegee—

Could that be Nolan Hoffsler?

Surely not...right?

After all, Janna didn't actually know the world-famous best-selling mystery writer. She'd only seen him interviewed on TV and online about his stories, including his most recent one that she'd read not long ago and really enjoyed.

He was far enough away that she couldn't really study his face, but he was handsome, with thick, dark hair and eyebrows and a sexy, pleased smile as he continued to hug Squeegee. And he should be pleased, since he had saved the dog from further trouble.

Janna told herself she was imagining things and hurried toward them. So what if it did turn out to be Hoffsler? Never mind that she admired the writer, partly because she aspired to be like him. After all, her passion, when she wasn't working in one of the veterinary clinics, was writing mysteries. She'd even finished a manuscript. Not that she'd sent it anywhere. Not yet, at least. She was still revising and polishing it.

"Thanks," she said when she reached them. Scott stood beside the man and dog as Janna knelt to snap a leash on Squeegee's collar. "He just ran out of the clinic on his bad leg, clearly hurting."

"Yeah, I noticed he was limping," the guy said as he rose.

Heck yes, he looked like Nolan Hoffsler. But what would he be doing here?

No, he was probably a guy in trouble seeking asylum here at the Chance Animal Shelter. People were often taken in as supposed staff members and protected even more than the stray animals. His resemblance to the noted author was most likely just Janna's imagination.

When the men started walking down the hall again, Janna bent to check on Squeegee's hurt paw. It was bandaged, and she saw no blood. However, now that the dog wasn't running, he sat with his right front paw held a bit off the floor.

"Come on, boy," Janna said softly. "Let's go back into the clinic, and I'll start working on treating that paw again. We'll walk slowly."

At the door to the shelter's veterinary clinic, she stopped and looked back down the hall. The men were no longer visible. They'd probably gone to Scott's office. Was Scott about to interview the man?

Well, just in case it was really Nolan Hoffsler, Janna would be sure to contact Scott later that afternoon and warn him about her suspicions, correct or not. If it really was Hoffsler, Scott could make sure the guy didn't do anything to publicize the Chance Animal Shelter and give away what it really did. The people under protection here could be put in danger by publicity.

Although if he was that novelist and just used the idea behind the shelter and set his story far, far away… Well, Scott should know the possibility, just in case, especially if he didn't know who Hoffsler was. Assuming it was him.

And if it was—well, she'd love to meet him. Maybe he could give her advice on her writing.

Janna led Squeegee slowly down the main hall of the clinic. She'd check on the other dogs here later. Her own dog, Wizzy, a highly trained Australian shepherd mix, was out on the grounds playing with some of the staff members. She almost always brought him to the shelter with her so he could have company. She'd go visit him soon, too.

For now, she just laughed at herself and her imagination—and silly writing ambition—as she lifted Squee-gee carefully and placed him on the examination table. Time to check that paw again.

Had the woman recognized him? Nolan wondered as Scott led him outside to another concrete building, this one with several floors.

"My office is upstairs," Scott told him as they entered the lobby. It wasn't particularly decorative but seemed nice enough. "Let's go on up." He pushed a button for an elevator, and one of the cars opened right away.

As they rose to the fourth floor, Nolan pondered the woman. Presumably she was a veterinarian or vet tech since she wore scrubs. She'd looked at him so keenly. Blonde, with green eyes—and a pretty tilt to her head as she seemed to study him.

If she had figured out who he was, so what? His face was out there a lot, after all, on his book covers and in the media as he was frequently interviewed to promote his books. He'd been quite successful, fortunately. At least so far.

But things might be changing now…

No matter. Scott knew who Nolan was and generally why he was there. Nolan was planning on giving him more specifics here in a bit.

As with his stories, Nolan had done his homework. Conducted what research he could to find a place where he would be able to stay as long as his life was in danger by a murderer.

As he always did when he was researching a story— and he never stopped—he observed and memorized his surroundings at Chance Animal Shelter here in Chance, California. Not that he could ever write about this place. He knew that. If it was all he believed it was, any publicity about it could harm the people who sheltered here.

Including, he hoped, himself. Soon. If all went well.

He was glad he'd heard rumors about this place while conducting research.

Scott led them past several offices, most likely belonging to other employees and managers at the shelter. At the end of the hall, he used a card to open the last door. Interesting that Scott didn't trust his own people enough to keep it open. Was he concerned that some of his staff would sneak up here and go through his things?

Not that there was a lot to go through. Yes, there was a nice-size metal desk with a computer. There were a few chairs. Behind the desk a placard on the wall had the Chance Animal Shelter logo on it, the same as on Scott's shirt.

"Have a seat." Scott gestured to the chairs in front of the desk.

Nolan had already studied him a bit, like he did with all people, places and things. Scott had short, dark hair and a bit of facial stubble, and he wore jeans along with his company shirt.

"Thanks," Nolan said. He sat down and took a deep breath, preparing to talk about stuff he enjoyed writing about—but hated experiencing himself. That was why he was here.

Before he could begin, Scott said, "From the way she reacted, I suspect Janna—our vet tech who recovered the dog—may have recognized you. In case she did, I'll talk to her later, whether or not we decide you can stay here. Either way, it's best if she doesn't mention seeing you, or someone like you."

"My thoughts exactly," Nolan agreed. "I'm used to getting recognized, and mostly that's a good thing. When I'm not in trouble. But now—"

"Now," Scott said, "let's talk about why you're here."

Okay. Time to face it. Nolan understood this was a place where people in trouble had to be accepted as new residents. If so, they were taken in for their protection. Like them, his life had been threatened.

Damn it. He needed to be accepted here at least until he was safe again.

And so, he took a deep breath and began telling his story, elaborating on the little he'd told Nolan before. It was both simple and complicated. "I travel a lot, but I mostly live in a nice neighborhood in San Diego. I'm generally home a lot—I write there and eat there and so on. But there's a restaurant I like not far from my home. Oddly, it's called Great Meals. I wouldn't say they're great, but they're definitely good enough to have lured me back a lot. Plus, I appreciated the owners. They were two friends, and their wives helped out at the place too. But last year—" Nolan hesitated.

Scott chimed in. "I heard about that even before you mentioned it to me. It was in the news a lot. One of the owners was murdered."

Nolan nodded. "That's right, Jaxon Draybell."

"And you told me that, as a mystery writer, you just had to write about it," Scott continued.

"My most recent novel is based on that particular

murder, but I did my own take on it. The co-owner, Declan Andershoot, was the chief suspect, but the evidence wasn't enough to take him into custody. Now the investigation has been ongoing for over a year. I was kind of hoping my new book, *Murder for Dinner*, would lead to them figuring out who did it or at least keep investigating it. Both wives, Luisa Draybell and Tanya Andershoot, seemed devastated, although they pretty much run the place now. Declan's mind was messed up from the trauma of the murder and being a suspect. I can't say I know him well, but I did believe him innocent, so I had to tell my own version of the story. I made it seem similar but different enough so it wouldn't appear that I believed I was stating what actually happened. After all, I don't write nonfiction."

"So who do you think did it?" Scott asked, clearly curious.

"Not sure," Nolan admitted. "I went to the restaurant often enough to recognize a lot of other patrons who enjoyed the place too. Sometimes I brought friends, and sometimes I came alone. I noticed now and then when other diners gave the owners some difficulty, but could any of them be the murderer? Who knows—although I did make one of the patrons the killer in my story." Not that Nolan had any evidence.

But he did have his imagination—and his reputation as a best-selling novelist. Those were good things. But what was bad…

"Interesting," Scott said, leaning over his desk a bit as he regarded Nolan with apparent interest. "And it makes sense. But you're here because…"

"Because, well, my book has been out for a couple of months. And once it was published, I started receiving death threats." Nolan swallowed hard, determined not to mention his fear, and continued, "I tried to ignore them since I sometimes do hear from nutcases who apparently read my mysteries. But...well, a month ago, my home was set on fire. Fortunately I noticed it quickly and called the fire department, who confirmed it had been deliberate. Not much damage was done, and I was fine. But—"

"But?" Scott prompted.

"But last week, as I was walking around my neighborhood, someone shot at me. They missed, but I didn't see who it was. I called the cops, but they didn't find anyone. I ignored the death threats, but setting my home on fire? Shooting at me? That I can't ignore."

Scott drew a little closer across the desk. "Who do you think it was?"

"I don't know, but I have to assume it was someone who feels threatened by my version of what happened and is seeking revenge. I can't stay in my home for now. That's why I'm here." Nolan paused, then said, "So can I stay at Chance Animal Shelter under protection for a while?"

"And you won't write about this place?"

"Absolutely not," Nolan said. "I could potentially jeopardize all your residents—including myself. Before I left home, I put out word on social media that I was heading to Pennsylvania, where I once lived, to make it as difficult as possible for my stalker to determine I'm here." He paused. "Assuming you accept me."

Scott's momentary silence felt like a slap in the face. Was Nolan about to be rejected?

"We'd have to work things out if you stayed," Scott finally said. "I assume you'll want to keep on writing, and that's fine as long as you bring your own computer. And when you first got in touch with me, you mentioned your need to stay in touch with certain people outside, which makes some sense. So, unlike most of our staff members here, you'd be permitted to communicate with the outside world on a limited basis, like checking your emails and responding to them, but only without indicating where you are or what you're up to."

Scott's intense expression told Nolan he expected a reply.

"No problem with that," Nolan said quickly. He paused. "I assume that communicating by phone would not be permitted, right?"

"Right, though in limited circumstances, if you need to actually talk to someone, we might be able to work something out—but not by using your own phone where someone might be able to determine your location by its GPS. We'd need to keep it for you, turned off, as you did for this visit."

"Makes sense," Nolan responded. "Look, Scott. The idea of being in a place like this is fascinating to me. It's something I most likely would have never thought of, even with my active imagination. Or I'd have stuck it in a story right away and rescued a whole lot of fictional people that way. But—well, fortunately, in conducting research on a story in the past, I heard how great the animal shelter was, and how nice it was to take in homeless people to care for the animals. But someone in law enforcement I talked to for research, and trust a lot, told me in confidence about some rumors about this place. I came to Chance just in case. And I guess the rumors are correct. I understand the reality. I never figured I'd need this kind of protection, but it's damned frightening to have someone I can't even identify threatening me this way—and trying to kill me. Guess I was just lucky, and I want to continue to be that way. I know I may not be the kind of person you really want to have here, but—"

"In some ways, you're exactly the kind of person we want here." Scott leaned back in his chair. "And it helps that you seem to be an intelligent guy in more ways than only your writing. If I accept you here, I need to be able to trust you." He paused, staring right into Nolan's eyes. "Can I?"

"Hell yeah," Nolan replied. "I've no idea how long I'll need to stay away from my real life, but the idea is to continue living. So tell me what promises you want from me, and I'll make them. And if I can't, I'll understand if you send me on my way—and I won't tell anyone about this place, in real life or a book."

Scott smiled now, and it seemed genuine. "Sounds good. We can talk a lot about what you can and can't do as time continues. But, Nolan Hoffsler, consider yourself a new staff member at the Chance Animal Shelter. Rather, Joshua—Josh—Forlett, welcome to our shelter. Everyone under protection here gets a new identity."

Josh Forlett. Nolan committed the name to memory. "Right. I'm Josh for now, and as long as I'm a resident here. Although you indicated I can still keep up my regular contacts by email, yes? I certainly won't reveal my new location or identity to anyone there."

"You've got it. And now, Josh, I'll give you the contract you'll need to sign to make sure you understand what you're getting into, including your promise of silence about the place. Then I'll show you to your new apartment, and afterward we'll go eat dinner in the cafeteria, so you can see how that works, as well as meet some of our managers and other staff members."

Nolan—Josh—took the contract Scott handed to him and read it carefully. It was important to know the contents of such things. He signed it and handed it back to Scott, who also signed at the bottom. He then handed a copy to Josh.

Josh rose and held out his hand. "Thanks, Scott. I can't tell you how much I appreciate this."

"Just keep all your promises and stay safe here, and that's thanks enough," Scott said, shaking his hand.

Josh smiled. Staying safe, and alive, was definitely his goal in coming here.

Chapter 2

Janna spent some time that afternoon working with the other animals in the clinic, including a little Pekingese mix named Pekie, a large retriever mix named Elmer, and a sleepy cat called Furball. None was in bad condition, fortunately, but just needed observation for minor injuries or listlessness. All appeared to be improving—including Squeegee. But it would be better if the pup didn't keep running on his injured paw.

She was about ready to leave the clinic for the day, but first she called Dr. Kyle Kornel, who was one of several veterinarians at the downtown Chance Animal Shelter. Janna had only been at Chance for a few months, but she knew he was a skilled vet and great to work for, which helped a lot. Plus, he'd once been a cop, which worked well for this shelter. Also, his girlfriend, Maisie Muran, was a K-9 cop. Every now and then, she visited the shelter with her dog.

"Hi, Janna." Kyle answered his phone right away, which meant he was in his office and not working with a patient at that moment. His day might be winding down too, although everyone working at the clinic was constantly on call in case of an emergency situation. And there was always a vet tech sleeping there each night.

But she was delighted that she had been chosen to be the sole vet tech, at least for now, to work at the Chance Animal Shelter almost every day, and sometimes stay here at night too, although so far, since she'd been working at the shelter, there'd been no veterinary emergencies overnight.

"Hi, Kyle," she said. "I've done what should be my last checks of the day for most of the animals here, although there's more of an issue with Squeegee." She described the pup's escape earlier that had aggravated his limp—without mentioning who had stopped him. Or, at least, who she thought had stopped him. "I'm going to stay here for dinner and check on him again."

"Good idea," Kyle replied. "Doesn't sound like he's too bad, but if you want to hang out there overnight, that could be a good thing. I'll be there tomorrow anyway, but I always feel better if one of us is around if there's an issue like that, even if it doesn't seem too serious."

"I might do that," Janna said. "And if not, I'll come here early tomorrow rather than heading to the downtown clinic first, okay?"

"Sure. See you one place or the other tomorrow, since I'll be there at the shelter for a while too."

"Great." They said their goodbyes and hung up. It was roughly dinnertime. She could eat here at the cafeteria and then come back and check on her patients again. That would be a good time to decide whether to stay the night or go home and return early tomorrow.

She couldn't help wondering—hoping—that she'd see

that guy in the cafeteria, whoever he might be. Maybe get to know him a little, flirt with him a bit. He was good-looking, after all, even if he wasn't who she hoped he was.

And if he did happen to be Hoffsler… Well, she'd just have to play things as they came up, to see if there was even the slightest possibility she could get his advice on her writing.

Of course, he might not be here any longer. Maybe he wasn't applying to become a staff member. Or maybe Scott hadn't approved him.

Anyway, time to stop pondering the guy and the situation.

Before she left the clinic to go to the cafeteria, she looked in on all the animals once more, checking that everyone had clean beds and blankets and water in their bowls. She put Squeegee into one of the more prominent spacious enclosures for dogs, near the front.

Now she could go check on her favorite animal of all, her own dog, Wizzy. She hoped someone was still playing with her pup out on the shelter grounds or reminding him of his training commands, but if not, they'd have put him in one of the enclosures in the building for medium-size dogs.

Fortunately, he wasn't alone. She found him inside that building. Chessie, a blond woman who seemed fairly young and dedicated to the dogs, was playing with him there. Like all other staff members, she wore a Chance Animal Shelter T-shirt. Today, hers was yellow.

"Hi, Janna," Chessie called. She held on as Wizzy, on a leash, began jumping toward Janna. "Someone seems glad to see you."

Laughing, Janna knelt and hugged her sweet, furry and obviously excited dog as he snuggled against her. "Hi, Wiz." She looked up at Chessie. "In case you can't tell, I'm glad to see him too."

This time Chessie laughed. "I figured. Are you on your way home now?"

"I'm going to have dinner here and then check again on Squeegee in the clinic to make sure his paw doesn't seem any worse."

"I'm about to head to the cafeteria too," Chessie said. "All three of us can walk there together."

"Sounds good." Not that it was far away. The cafeteria was on the ground floor of a building nearby, with apartments above. Nothing at this shelter was far from anything else. But it was large enough, with its tall fencing, to protect quite a few people in trouble as well as dozens of animals needing new homes.

Janna, Chessie and Wizzy passed the building for small dogs and headed back toward the welcome area, offices and apartments.

And they weren't the only ones streaming into the cafeteria. It was six o'clock, just when dinner was being served.

A few staff members were already sitting at the long tables, but more were standing in line for the food served along one wall. Janna wasn't surprised to see Sara standing there watching and apparently making suggestions. From what Janna had learned about her, Sara wasn't too interested in working with the animals, but she loved cooking, so she'd been put in charge of food preparation. Why was that attractive but reserved middle-aged lady here at the shelter? Janna didn't know but figured she'd had a hard life outside, like everyone else.

Everybody seemed glad to see Wizzy. Janna had permission to bring her pup to the cafeteria, mostly so she could have him with her since she spent so much time in the clinic. Pretty much all the staff members liked animals, especially dogs, since that was one of the prerequisites to their being accepted here. To the world outside, they were supposedly homeless folks hired to help out by caring for the animals at this respected animal shelter.

No way could it be publicized that they were here for their own protection, despite some outsiders, mostly authorities, aware of it.

"Hi, Wizzy," said Augie, who waited ahead of them in line. The senior had just a bit of dark hair left on his head, and he had to exert some effort to bend over to pet her dog. But he seemed determined, and Janna found that cute.

"He says hi back," she told the man when he smiled up at her.

Sara beckoned for Augie to move down the line. "Your turn."

As Janna waited her turn, she bent again to pat her dog between the ears. When she stood up, she glanced toward her favorite table on the other side of the room. Scott and his girlfriend, Nella, usually sat there. Nella was the assistant director at the shelter. Janna didn't know her background, but she seemed to do a great job as Scott's backup. The pretty woman looked good as always, sitting at the table in her black Chance Animal Shelter T-shirt.

Janna noticed Scott heading toward Nella…along with the man who'd been in her mind all day. She assumed that, with Scott accompanying him, he'd be sitting at that main table.

Would there be room for her? Scott and Nella usually were fine with her joining them, but a lot of people liked to. Janna would need to hurry, although she still needed to get her food. On the other hand, she'd apparently arrived early enough that there were still lots of spots available for other people to sit, despite the line.

Keeping Wizzy's leash looped around her wrist, Janna picked up a plate and began filling it as she followed Augie at the food table. The meal smelled amazing: a stew of some kind that had small meatballs in it and a lot of veggies. She was happy to see a salad on the side. She wasn't a vegetarian, but she didn't like to eat a lot of meat.

Wizzy, on the other hand, ate plenty of meat, both kibble and canned, as well as fresh pet meals sometimes. It was what she recommended to anyone asking what they should feed their dogs. Quality counted. Tonight, she'd probably give her pup a few meatballs—and yes, some veggies too.

After filling her plate, Janna walked toward Scott and Nella's table. "Come," she told Wizzy. She would pick up a drink once she got her seat figured out.

She wanted to clap since a few empty seats remained at the long table. Maybe she should even cheer since one of those seats was next to the newcomer she wanted to talk to.

Would he be okay with her sitting next to him? After

all, her staring earlier hadn't exactly made it a secret that she thought she knew who he was. But their conversation, if he talked with her, could really be interesting.

"Hi, Nella," Janna said as she reached the table. "Hi, Scott. Okay if I join you?"

"Sure," Nella said. "How about there?" She gestured toward the seat Janna hoped for, which made her smile. "There's room for Wizzy to sit on the floor beside you."

"Perfect," Janna said, not mentioning the other reason she found it perfect. But she glanced toward the newcomer as if asking for his okay too. His smile didn't look as big as the one she felt on her own face, but neither did he say no.

"Janna, I'd like you to meet our new staff member," Scott said. "I know you met before when he helped you catch Squeegee. This is Josh. And Josh, this is our vet tech Janna Welles."

"Glad to meet you," Janna said.

"Glad to meet you too," he replied. He now wore one of the Chance Animal Shelter T-shirts, in navy blue. "And I hope that dog you were chasing is okay."

"Squeegee is fine, partly thanks to you."

He turned back to Scott, whom he'd been conversing with.

Janna turned to Nella. "Could I speak with you for a second? I have a question relating to the vet clinic." Actually, that wasn't what she wanted to talk about right now. But getting that close to "Josh" and seeing his face once more…

"Sure." Nella stood and moved around the table.

Janna set her food down and led Wizzy over to the windows looking out at the courtyard.

"What's up?" Nella's pretty brown eyes narrowed in apparent concern.

And what Janna wanted to say could certainly be concerning. "I… I just wanted to let you and Scott know that I believe I recognize Josh. I assume he's now a staff member, right?"

"That's right," Nella said.

"Well, he may be a famous author who gets a lot of publicity—which I know you don't want here. I figured I'd better let you know my suspicions, in case he didn't tell you and is here to research a story or something. He might let out information that shouldn't be revealed."

"Got it," Nella said. "And thanks for your concern and letting us know about it. But you can feel certain we've vetted Josh well as we do everyone here. We'll remain careful, of course, and I'll let Scott know what you've said. But you don't need to worry about it."

"Great," Janna said. Maybe the guy wasn't Nolan after all? Or in his interview, had he somehow convinced Scott that he wouldn't tell the world about this place even in a story?

If so, Janna hoped he'd told the truth.

Had that been about him? Josh wondered. Both Nella and Janna glanced at him before returning to the table from their brief conversation. Was Janna warning Nella about who she thought he was?

Well, so what? Scott and Nella knew everything already. He'd just have to be careful around the vet tech.

Or maybe even talk to her if the time seemed right. He was here to hide, and he certainly didn't want someone asking questions about Nolan Hoffsler and whether he was around this shelter.

For now, as the women rejoined them, he rose again to be polite. "Guess we're going to be tablemates tonight, Janna, which will hopefully be fun."

He noticed that she had changed clothes, or at least taken off her vet scrubs jacket. Now, he could see how her T-shirt and scrub pants hugged her body. He'd not considered veterinary scrubs particularly sexy before, but they sure looked that way on her.

On the other hand, her quizzical gaze made him more uncomfortable than sexually aroused.

It was probably better that way.

"I hope so, Josh." She stressed his new name, or was he just imagining that since he suspected she knew who he really was? "I'd been hoping to see you this evening since I'd wanted to express again how grateful I was that you helped stop Squeegee before he hurt himself even more."

"No problem," he said. Although if she possibly recognized him…? Well, she was one of the people who worked here, apparently. That meant Scott and Nella must trust her. Hopefully, he would be able to trust her too.

Was Janna her real name…? Well, as far as he knew so far, the vets and technicians were outsiders, not staff members.

The dog that came in with Janna had remained at her side on a leash and now settled on the floor beside her as she took her seat next to him.

"This tastes really good," he told her as he also sat back down. "I hadn't realized there'd be a cafeteria where all staff members were invited to eat."

"Then you are a new staff member?" she asked, looking him in the eyes.

"Definitely. Scott accepted me this afternoon. In fact, he showed me my new apartment before bringing me here for dinner."

It was a nice enough apartment —small but adequate, with reasonable furnishings. Scott had left him there for about twenty minutes to get settled in and change into one of his new Chance Animal Shelter T-shirts before dinner.

He'd wondered if this lovely vet tech would be at the cafeteria. Did she live at the shelter like the staff members? Like him now? He'd figured he might see her again sometime since she must come to care for the animals in the veterinary clinic. And he'd wondered if it would be a good thing to see her again so quickly.

Oh, yes, he enjoyed looking at the pretty woman, even speaking with her. But would she endanger his confidentiality here? He certainly hoped not. After all, everyone connected with this place had to know how secret it was, and how important it was not to let the world know anything about its residents.

Janna was giving her dog small pieces of stew. "Well, I hope you like the apartment." She looked back up at Josh. "And the food in this cafeteria. I hope all goes well for you here as a new staff member." There was an inquisitive look on her face that suggested she was trying to see through his skull and into his brain to decipher who this new staffer really was. The writer she apparently thought he was?

He wasn't about to tell her. If he ever needed to tell her anything, he'd use the backstory he and Scott had discussed. In fact, it wouldn't hurt to mention it now.

"I'm sure it will," he said, then leaned toward her and spoke softly as he lied. "In case you're wondering—and I know we're not supposed to talk about such things— I came here because of a particularly nasty family incident."

He looked her in the face as her expression grew dubious—but still didn't turn her into anything but beautiful. "Yes, I was wondering," she said, also keeping her voice low. "Thanks for letting me know."

Okay, he had little doubt that she really did recognize him. Regardless he hoped to see more of her here—and maybe he could use her as a research source someday for a future murder mystery that involved a vet tech.

"So how did you get into being a veterinary technician?" he asked. Would she say anything that was mystery-worthy? For the moment, it didn't matter. He was actually interested.

She gave a brief laugh, as she apparently recognized what he was trying to do—change the subject. "That's a fun story," she said. "Would you believe I've always loved animals?"

"Really? Now, that surprises me." He chuckled. "So tell me more."

Chapter 3

Okay, "Josh" wasn't going to tell her the truth, Janna figured. Maybe it was because of where they were. Although no one at their crowded table seemed to pay attention beyond their own conversations, someone could be listening. It wasn't only Scott and Nella who sat around them, but also the other managers, blond-bearded Campbell Green and thirtyish Telma Andelson, along with staff members including Augie and Veronica, who was relatively new, petite and middle-aged.

Whoever Josh was, for whatever reason he was really there, he was right. This wasn't the time or place to discuss it—never mind the bit of his story that was most likely given to him along with his new name.

But Janna could tell him a bit of her own story here. Maybe that would lure him into talking, too, at a different location later. Not that she wanted to breach anyone's sense of privacy and secrecy, especially at this shelter. Maybe she could somehow let him know that, whether or not he was who she believed he was. And she already felt fairly certain he was.

She took a sip of water first, then bent to give Wizzy another little meatball. She didn't want to overdo it, but when she looked down at her pup, his begging stare made denial impossible. As it often did.

Then she looked back at Josh—and enjoyed the handsome view again. "When I was about twelve years old growing up in Phoenix," she began, raising her voice a little to be heard over the crowd, "I was playing catch with some friends in a park near my home. My big brother, Alan, who was fourteen then, was with me. He tossed the ball too far, toward some trees—and when I got there, I found a puppy lying in a pile of leaves."

"Poor thing," Josh said. "Was it okay?"

"Well, I didn't know much about dogs then, but it was a little Chihuahua mix. It clearly was in pain, the way it was writhing. I obviously couldn't just leave it but knew enough to be concerned about picking it up, so I found a big piece of cardboard to carefully put it on and got Alan to help me. We found some adults there—one of the kids' parents—and they helped us take the pup to a nearby veterinarian."

"Glad to hear that," Josh said.

"I was too. Fortunately the vet was a nice lady and took over helping the pup. Alan called our parents and— well, the upshot was that the pup had apparently been attacked by a larger dog and survived. Our parents could tell how much I cared, so they paid the vet for her treatment and, after trying unsuccessfully to find her owner, we wound up adopting her. We called her Wonderful or Wonny."

"Cute."

"And I'd no idea, at my age then, how much it cost to get her cured. But when I was older, I was told the vet,

Dr. Evaston, reduced the cost under the circumstances. When we were ready to take Wonny home, I asked Dr. Evaston if I could help save other animals. She let me come back after school a couple days a week to feed and walk some of the dogs in her care—well, I was hooked." Janna felt she'd gone on too long about herself, so before Josh could say anything, she asked, "How about you? I gather you like dogs too. Did you have any as pets?"

She didn't think he put any animals into his mysteries, or at least none she had read. That was probably a good thing. People got hurt a lot in his books, and that wouldn't be right for animals, not even fictional ones.

"I don't have any now," he said, "but I had a black Labrador retriever named Duke for years. And when he was gone—well, that was so painful I haven't wanted to get another one."

"I understand," she said. "Although you now know a veterinary technician who could help you with your new canine baby's care." She grinned.

"Yeah. I do think often about getting another dog but just haven't done it."

"Maybe you'll fall in love with one here at the shelter," Janna said. "I always advise people to adopt pets from places like this."

"I like that idea. And—"

"Hey, Josh," said Augie at his other side. Josh turned, and Augie engaged him in conversation.

Their own conversation was over for now, but Janna had enjoyed it, even though it had been more about her than him. Hopefully, it was just the start. There were more things she wanted to discuss. For now, Janna glanced at the others nearby.

Nella was next to her, talking to Scott who sat on her other side. Bibi, a staffer who had been at the shelter since before Janna came here as a vet tech, was chatting with Veronica beside her. Bibi was known for her good care and training of shelter animals. She glanced toward Janna, who smiled back at her.

"Everything okay with Squeegee?" Bibi asked, looking very concerned suddenly. "Is his leg getting better?"

Janna always enjoyed talking about the animals she cared for in the clinic—particularly when they all seemed to be doing fairly well. In between moments of conversation, she continued to eat, sip water, give a little food to Wizzy…and glance frequently at Josh.

Judging by Josh's questions to Augie, he seemed interested in joining the staff soon in their duties. For research on whatever his latest project was?

Okay, she had to stop thinking like that. The man had been accepted as a staff member. Whoever he was, he was undoubtedly in trouble in some way, family or whatever.

Could a famous author like Nolan Hoffsler be in that kind of situation?

Well, who couldn't?

Eventually, Janna noted that everyone around her, including Josh, appeared to be finishing their meals. She started to stand, and so did Wizzy, sidling up to her right leg. "Great eating with you all tonight," she said. "I'm going to go back to the clinic to check on our patients." She glanced at Josh. "What are you up to this evening, newbie?"

"Not sure yet. Could I join you to see your clinic? I'd like to see how you take care of the animals."

"That's fine." Janna half expected other staffers to ask to come along, but they were all absorbed in their own conversations. Good. She probably wouldn't have said no, but she figured being alone in the clinic with Josh might give her an opportunity to ask him questions.

She wasn't surprised when Josh stopped to talk briefly with Scott and let him know he'd be heading to his apartment soon. He thanked the director without saying expressly why, but Janna understood that Josh was happy to have been accepted as a staffer here, for whatever *real* reason he was seeking help.

"I assume I should show up here at breakfast tomorrow," Josh said, "and that I'll be given my duties at the shelter?"

"That's right." Nella smiled approvingly, standing beside Scott. "I'll be here then and can get you working with other staff members who already know the routine, which dogs to walk and train when. They'll bring you onboard."

"Sounds perfect." Josh shook hands first with Nella, then with Scott. Janna was amused to see other staffers looking on, smiling and laughing. One couple even clapped.

"Welcome to your new home, Josh," Bibi said, and a few others echoed, "Yes, welcome."

He appeared genuinely grateful and thanked them all. No matter who he was, Janna reflected, he was now a staff member here and seemed prepared to act like one. And hopefully not do anything to undermine this place or its purpose. Janna respected Scott. If he believed in this guy, then Janna had to as well.

Still, she could get to know him better and see what she could learn—without breaking the rules too much about prying into a resident's background.

Not too much was the key.

"So," Janna finally said after everyone near them had welcomed Josh, "are you ready to visit the clinic with me?"

"Absolutely," he said. "I may not be as involved with animals as you, but as you may have gathered, I really care about them. Or why else would I be here?" He smiled at her.

The dazzling look with his deep brown eyes might have mesmerized her, if she hadn't been a bit suspicious about everything he said. "Oh, I suspect there may be other reasons," she said, then motioned to him while tightening her grip on Wizzy's leash. "Let's go."

They bussed their items from the table, leaving their dishes with the staff designated to wash up after today's meal. As they walked, they passed a few other staffers. Had Josh met them yet? Well, Janna wasn't about to introduce them now.

Instead, she led him from the cafeteria and outside to the building where the clinic was located, with Wizzy accompanying them. Josh held the door for her and her pup, then walked next to her down the hall to the clinic.

"Did you have to wait long when you first arrived before someone came to get you?" Janna asked. She suspected that, if Josh was who she believed, he might have been considered too important to leave for long in the welcome area's entry.

"No," Josh said. "Scott had someone come out to meet me right away."

At the clinic's door, Janna paused to unlock it. They couldn't have residents coming in to play with or otherwise bother the animals needing veterinary care. The drugs inside were also kept separately locked, even though the meds kept wouldn't necessarily be appealing or even useful to humans. But she was glad no one would be able to test that.

"I'm going to leave Wizzy here in lobby while we visit the patients," Janna told Josh.

She closed the door behind them, then led Josh down the short hall to the enclosures for animals receiving care. Janna headed for Squeegee, peeking at the others as she passed but not stopping until she reached the dog she was most concerned about.

She opened the mesh door of the enclosure and let Squeegee out. Unsurprisingly, he limped.

"Poor boy," she said. "Let's go into the exam room so I can check you out."

"Would you like me to carry him?" Josh asked.

That was sweet—and probably also an indication of how strong he was.

"Thanks, but not yet, at least. I want to see how he does when he walks."

The limp seemed neither better nor worse. When they got inside the well-equipped exam room, she did ask Josh to lift Squeegee onto the metal-topped table. Not that she couldn't have done it herself, but she wanted to see this man use those muscles, no matter how briefly or unnecessarily.

She made sure she didn't smile as she observed his biceps flex as he lifted the pup.

Okay, this was ridiculous. Yes, he was a good-looking man, whether or not he resembled—or was—her writing idol. But it was totally inappropriate for her to feel at all attracted to him. Whoever he was, he was an official staff member here at the shelter, which meant he was under protection. And not hers.

She got down to her job, which she loved. "Thanks," she told Josh, then bent toward Squeegee. "Hi, boy. How's that paw? I need to look at it."

The pup regarded her with his large brown eyes as if trying to decipher what she'd said but didn't pull back when she lifted his leg. She gently removed the bandage and looked at the area beneath. It still appeared somewhat raw, but no worse than previously. Squeegee had apparently been bitten badly by another dog before being brought into the shelter.

"Is he okay?" Josh asked.

"Maybe a little better, so I can hope he's healing. But fortunately my boss, Dr. Kornel, will be here tomorrow and can check it out."

"I know you're a vet tech and not a vet," Josh said, "but I bet you know what you're doing."

"Thanks," she said, feeling her face redden. "And you're absolutely right." Enough of that. "Okay, boy," she said to Squeegee. "Let's walk just a little." They did keep him confined some at the clinic, but didn't want him to lose his mobility.so they let him walk quite a bit.

She didn't wait for Josh to lift the dog down from the table but did it herself, gently placing him on the floor. She looked up at Josh almost defiantly to find he was grinning.

"I guess vet techs have to be strong," he said.

"This one's strong enough. Now let's go, Squeegee."

They began walking slowly down the hallway. Josh stood near the door to the exam room, watching them. Squeegee continued to limp, as anticipated. Janna wished she could do something magical to heal the poor pup's paw immediately, but of course she couldn't.

She hoped Dr. Kornel would be able to do something about it tomorrow. Maybe he'd have some new way of improving it, but she doubted it. Time would just have to pass as the paw improved.

Back in the exam room, she placed the pup on the table once more, again doing it herself, then washed the area carefully with antiseptic, placed a bit of ointment on it, then rebandaged it.

"Okay, Squeegee," she said. "Time for you to rest again."

Before she could move, Josh came over and picked the dog up. "Do you want me to carry him?"

"That would be great," Janna said. She'd probably have done the same thing rather than making Squeegee walk again for now, so Josh's help was quite welcome. She led the way back to Squeegee's wire enclosure. His fluffy dog bed seemed fine, and there were some chew toys on the floor, as well as a full bowl of water.

With Josh at her side, she checked on Pekie and Elmer and Furball, taking them out of their enclosures, talking to them, quickly examining them and making sure they didn't seem any worse than previously.

"Okay, babies," she said. "Dinnertime." Her turn tonight, although they sometimes had shelter staffers do it under manager observation.

Josh helped dish some kibble and canned food into the three dog bowls as well as some specialized cat food for Furball. He talked to the animals as he fed them, clearly enjoying their presence.

Good guy, she thought.

When the animals were finished eating, she removed their bowls and cleaned them. No one's health seemed to require that she pop in again to check on them that night, not even Squeegee's, even though she was hanging out at the apartment here designated for the vet clinic tonight. Time to leave.

But she had a thought about how to stay with Josh a bit longer.

"I'm heading to the clinic's apartment now," she told him. "And I know it has a couple bottles of beer, if you'd like to join me."

"Sure," he said. "Sounds good."

"Oh, and there is a television, but I've also got a lot of books there. I love to read. How about you?" How would he react to that?

"Yes," he said. "I get along with books even better than I do with animals. That's probably why I've got a bunch of books but no pets."

"Good," she said. "We can talk about what we like to read best as we drink our beer."

He gave a brief laugh. "Sound like a great way to end the evening."

She retrieved Wizzy from the clinic's lobby and took a bit of time on the walk to the apartment to let him do what he needed, with Josh following.

Janna couldn't help looking around as they headed back toward the cafeteria and the apartment units upstairs. No one was outside. Good. It might not be appropriate for her to bring one of the staff members to the clinic's apartment, so it was better if they weren't seen.

But it was a risk she was willing to take. She was looking forward to enjoying a beer with him—and talking about books.

Josh found the situation amusing and intriguing... and worrisome as he followed Janna into the apartment building.

He presumed they would be alone in Janna's apartment, which would be fine. He would behave himself, not do anything inappropriate, no matter how much this lovely vet tech attracted him.

But she had mentioned books. She seemed to know who he was from the first time they'd met. Were they going to get into a conversation about his background?

He should probably just lie and maintain the identity Scott had given him. That was the rule around here, after all. He would just have to be careful. And strong. Like one of the protagonists in his books, who got into situations where murders had been committed and solved them, always coming out safely and in control.

They passed the cafeteria on the ground floor and approached a set of stairs. "I assume someone who can just pick up largish dogs like Squeegee is okay with walking upstairs," Janna said. "My unit's on the next floor anyway."

"Sounds good. Let's walk it."

Josh followed Janna and Wizzy up the stairs to a hallway of apartments. Janna used a key to open the fourth door on the right.

The place resembled the one Scott had shown him earlier as his new habitat. All the apartments probably looked similar. The living room had a gray sofa just like the one in his place plus a couple of chairs with a coffee table in front of them. The floor was wood laminate. A television was mounted on one wall. Not a particularly glamorous dwelling. Not that it needed to be. He gathered this was just the place clinic staff stayed when they had to be around overnight.

"This way," she said, motioning him to follow her into the kitchen. A dog bowl sat on the beige tile floor, with just a little water in it.

Josh picked it up, dumped out the residue in the sink and refilled it.

"Hey, Wizzy and I thank you," Janna said, her smile lighting up her beautiful face in a way that made him want to draw closer to her. After all, they were alone here in her apartment. But they'd just met, so he stayed where he was, watching as Janna extracted two bottles of a nice quality imported beer from the stainless steel refrigerator.

The woman had good taste, although he wasn't surprised.

As Wizzy drank from his bowl, Janna got a bottle opener from a drawer near the metal sink, then sat down on one of the wooden chairs at the kitchen table. She motioned for Josh to do the same, which he did.

"So where's your apartment?" she asked.

"A couple of floors above here," he replied. "It looks a lot like this one."

"I figured," she said. "They're all similar." She took a swig of her beer and closed her eyes for a moment as if in ecstasy, which made a certain part of him react. Would she look that way if they—

"So tell me," she said, opening her eyes and staring directly into his. "Okay, I know this isn't appropriate, but I am 99% sure you're the mystery author Nolan Hoffsler. What got you started writing mysteries and thrillers?"

Here we go, he thought. How was he going to handle this?

Chapter 4

Josh didn't answer right away. Janna wasn't surprised. If he had, she figured he would deny he was a writer, Nolan or not.

"In case I didn't make it clear to you before," she said to encourage him after taking another sip of her beer, "I love reading." She kept looking into those deep brown eyes of his, but they remained somewhat bland, as if he didn't want her to get any hint of what he was thinking. Or was there a hint of amusement in them? Either way, she found his expression unexpectedly stimulating. Because she wanted him to finally admit who he was? Despite feeling attracted to him, she knew seduction by either of them certainly wouldn't work. Would it?

Would she even consider letting things go that way if he wasn't Hoffsler?

"And I love writing," she continued. "In fact, Nolan Hoffsler's stories are among my favorites. The manuscript I've been working on is a romantic suspense story that includes a murder mystery, kind of what the professionals would consider a mixed genre, more crime fiction than cozy, somewhat of a thriller, with a cop as a protagonist. It doesn't imitate any of Hoffsler's stories, but I'd say that the mixed genre is similar, although the romances in his aren't the focus."

"Sounds interesting," he said. "But think of your remaining one percent uncertainty. I've read a lot of Hoffsler's books and think they're quite good. Stuff I'd like to have written if I wrote."

Of course he would have read all of them But she felt frustrated that he wasn't admitting anything and clenched her fists behind her back for an instant.

"So is your writing good like that?" he asked, drinking some more beer.

"My only manuscript so far is somewhat like that," she reiterated. He nodded and drank some more beer. "And is it any good?"

She took a deep breath. "I think it's damn good." She hoped. What would Hoffsler think of it? She had to find out—but first, she needed to confirm her suspicions.

"I told you why I became a vet tech," she said, staring straight at him. "And, well, I figured it wouldn't be appropriate not to tell you who I thought you really are. And I definitely admire you. I'd really like for you to tell me how you decided to start writing. When you started. How you decided it was time to try to get your first story published. It was with one of the big-name publishers, of course, although I don't remember which one." Okay, she thought. Was he going to deny it?

"I'm flattered that you'd ask me all that and assume I'm as good, and famous, a writer as Nolan Hoffsler— not that I'd admit it if I was. Look, as I said I've read a lot of his work. If you'd like to show me whatever you've written, I'd be delighted to read it and give you my comments. I can't promise they'd be useful, but maybe they'd help."

Wonderful. No confirmation or clarification. No anything except that this man admitted he'd read Hoffsler's books and was willing to critique her writing. A good idea either way? Who knew?

She took a deep breath, still staring at that gorgeous face of his. "Look, I know I'm not supposed to inquire about your background since you're now a staff member here under protection, but—"

"You're right. And I've been told not to talk about my past to anyone except the managers here. Even though you're not another staff member, I think that includes you, and I did let you know what I was allowed to mention."

His stare didn't waver—although it seemed to grow more sexy somehow. Okay. She worked here part-time and did need to obey the rules. But sometimes staff members told others at least something about their actual backgrounds, not just the stories they'd been given.

As much as she wanted to keep watching him, she finally looked away. Maybe she could try to convince him to tell her who he was by… Well, what? Trying to seduce him?

No way.

"Fine," she said, finally looking away. "I don't have any critique partners since this is new to me. I guess it wouldn't hurt to have a stranger who happens to like the same books comment on my manuscript. But we'll have to figure out when and where you can read it so that no one else will learn about it or see it or—"

Her throat tightened with emotion, and she didn't

finish. But they looked each other in the eyes and both stood up, and suddenly she found herself in Josh's arms.

"I get it," he said in a rough whisper. "We're all keeping secrets here, and I'll keep yours."

Where did that closeness—physically and emotionally— come from? She didn't care. She loved his grip, and when she looked up into his eyes again, his mouth came down on hers.

Their kiss was long and sexy and definitely inappropriate. Whoever this man was, he was a staff member here. But she certainly enjoyed it. And felt sad when it ended. Still, she didn't want him to know how much it affected her.

Wizzy had drawn closer, maybe to protect her, and Janna bent to give him a brief pat between the ears.

"Wow," she said, stepping back and smiling into Josh's face. How did he look even sexier now? "Are you trying to distract me, Mr. Hoffsler?"

He laughed. "Okay, I'm not admitting to anything, and that may not have been a good idea, but it felt damned good to me." Before she could say ditto, he was the one to step farther away. "Look, I need to get back to my apartment. And I've already told you what brought me here, to the Chance Animal Shelter. Ugly family stuff."

Was that the truth, or just what he'd been told to say?

"Oh, right," she said.

"And I'd like to at least read some of your manuscript tonight before I go to sleep."

She smiled. She liked the idea, since she hadn't gotten over the idea he was who she believed.

"Sure," she said. "It's on my computer, of course, but I also have a printed version I could give to you, and it would be fine if you jotted notes on it. Would that be okay? Oh, and don't show anyone else or tell them about it. As you probably figured out, I'm being fairly secretive about it for now." Except for mentioning it to a couple people she was somewhat close to here, plus a complete stranger who might—or might not—be a famous author.

"Yes, I did figure that. And that sounds fine to me."

She considered asking him to spend the night here to start that reading, but she realized how bad an idea that was. Hopefully no one would see him leave here tonight, but having him around in the morning might make it even more likely he'd be seen.

And spending the night… Well, the possibilities that passed quickly through her mind were intriguing but included more than him reading her story. A lot more, considering how appealing this man was.

And that couldn't happen.

"I'll go get it." She went into the bedroom—alone. She spent the most time here and had a small desk in there with her computer and printer on it. She pulled the manuscript out of a desk drawer where she hid it and put it in an expandable folder. Then, from some shelves near the bed, she selected a book.

She returned to the kitchen and handed Josh the folder. "Here. I'll be really interested in what you think of it." Then she held up the old paperback she'd brought out. It was a Nolan Hoffsler mystery that she left at this apartment so clinic staff could read it on any nights they were here—and the author's picture was inside the back cover.

Janna opened it and looked from the photo to Josh and back again. "Hmm," she said. "If you're not him, you might be his twin brother."

He looked at the picture as if it was new to him. "I see what you mean. I've seen the resemblance when I've read some of his books too."

"Some of *your* books," she contradicted. "Never mind. I understand your need for confidentiality. And I certainly won't say anything to anyone else." Other than those she wanted to know about it to protect this shelter.

But she wished he'd finally admit it to her, just because she wanted to know.

Well, maybe when he critiqued her manuscript.

He didn't say anything else but bent to give Wizzy a pat, then looked back up into Janna's face. He didn't draw closer, though, and she stopped herself from going to give him a goodnight kiss.

"See you in the morning," he said. "Hopefully we can eat breakfast together. I'll leave your manuscript in my apartment till I finish reading it, and we can figure out a good time to discuss it and let me give it back to you."

"Sounds good." Janna ignored her wistfulness as she accompanied him to the door. "Do you know how to get to your apartment?" She'd go along with him if necessary, even though that would again make it more obvious to anyone around that they'd been together.

"Definitely. Good night." He bent his head and gave her a quick kiss on the lips. Then he patted Wizzy on the head once more and left.

She couldn't help feeling hopeful—and confused. She would look forward to his comments, since no one else had read any of her material. But she didn't like the idea that she was attracted to him. Whether he was Hoffsler or not, it was inappropriate.

"Come on, Wizzy," she said to her dog, going into the kitchen to get his leash. "We're going for a walk."

Inside the grounds of the shelter. But they'd at least get a little exercise. Maybe that would tire her out enough to be able to sleep well.

Maybe.

Josh looked around as he left Janna's apartment, making sure no one would spot him. He'd already come up with some excuses for being there, like bringing her something from the clinic she'd left behind—maybe a toy of Wizzy's or some bandages that had fallen from her pocket.

Fortunately, he didn't see anyone, not along the stairway or in the fourth floor hall. His apartment was the last one on the left. At the door, he shifted the bulky file folder in his arms and reached into his pocket for his key card, trying to remain quiet. At least at this apartment, he wouldn't have to explain to anyone what he was doing. For now this was his home, and he really had no interest in speaking to anyone else for the rest of the night.

Anyone else. If he'd remained with Janna, or if she'd accompanied him here… No, that was just a bad idea.

He opened the door and walked inside, looking around. The place was definitely similar to Janna's unit.

For a moment, he kind of wished he had a dog to keep him company, like Wizzy. Maybe he could temporarily take in one of the dogs here at the shelter—adding to its training and ability to bond with humans. He'd keep that in mind.

He made sure the door was securely fastened behind him—not that he figured anyone would follow him in here. No threats were likely to follow him here, on the secure grounds of Chance Animal Shelter.

It was getting late. He would like to have grabbed another beer, but there wasn't much in his fridge, just a container of water and some food he'd been told had already been placed into his apartment —bread and cheese and sliced turkey, in case he wanted to eat a sandwich here sometime. And he wasn't really hungry now, even though a bit of time had passed since dinner.

But he didn't plan to go to bed soon. He wanted to read Janna's manuscript, or as much of it as he could before falling asleep.

He settled onto the sofa with a glass of water and turned on a lamp beside him. He pulled the pages out of the folder—then stood and went into his bedroom for the writing supplies he'd stuffed into his suitcase in the hopes he would be accepted here: an empty spiral notebook with lined paper and a pen.

He'd make notes on Janna's pages, if necessary. But if he saw anything major to suggest to her, he'd jot it down in his notebook.

Then he began reading. And enjoying.

Oh, sure, she wasn't a veteran, with her occasional grammar flubs and fuzziness in a few descriptions. But considering that he was probably the first critic she was running it by, he was impressed.

It was definitely a romance, about a woman who owned a coffee shop in a small town where lots of people came to sit and enjoy their java. But Janna had added some characters who seemed quiet and kept to themselves. One guy had just come to town, and the protagonist was intrigued by his apparent background in the military—but it was unclear what he did now. As it turned out, he was undercover FBI trying to ferret out what the other coffee drinkers were up to—since they seemed to be plotting something evil that could harm the whole town.

And there was more to it than that. Janna had done a good job building the intrigue—and his interest. Her descriptions were mostly well crafted. Her characters well developed. And the romance…

If he'd been curious about what Janna knew about lovemaking, he didn't wonder any longer. He smiled as he read what was probably just the first sex scene—and utterly stimulating—in an early chapter of the manuscript.

He was amused that she would want him to read this. After all, they'd been flirting at least a little. Did she want him to think about her when he read about the hero and heroine jumping into bed together and enjoying themselves?

The thought of sex with Janna had certainly entered his mind, no matter how inappropriate. And reading what she had written about lovemaking made his insides—and some of his outside—stir.

No matter. He had no intention of mentioning the sex scenes in his critique. It was the characters and plot that would determine whether what she'd written was publishable. The sex scenes could always be modified by editors when the story was bought for publication in the future.

And he had a sense that this story was definitely publishable.

Oh, it wasn't at the level of his bestsellers. But he'd had to start somewhere too. His first stories had been good, sure. But he'd gotten even better over time.

Time. It was getting late. He was getting tired.

He checked the page count. He still had nearly three quarters of the manuscript left to read. But he hadn't wanted to simply scan it. He had made some notes about parts he thought could be handled better. But on the whole, he liked it. He had some thoughts about it, yes, but he wouldn't need to be too critical.

And if he found some alone time with Janna tomorrow, he could start discussing it with her then and finish reading it later.

Alone time. That sounded both good and concerning—but he'd figure it out.

For now, he wanted to get on his computer before heading to bed and check a few things. He needed to see who might have attempted to contact Nolan Hoffsler.

His current editor had sent an email to ask when to expect the next manuscript, which almost made him smile. Almost. Oh, he'd been plotting something mostly in his mind, but he wasn't sure when he'd be able to even start actually writing it. Hopefully he'd at least be able to add to his notes for it tomorrow.

For now, he wrote back that he'd been working on it and would be sending something soon. Although *soon* was probably quite some time away... Fortunately, he was successful enough—and made the publisher enough revenue—that he could be vague about timing.

And he did definitely intend to get back to writing when he could clear his mind a bit. Well, a lot. Hopefully, at this shelter, he would soon no longer feel in so much danger.

He next checked some of his social media accounts. Fans were still saying nice things about his latest release, as they also tended to do about prior books he'd published.

Fortunately, as with email, the location of the person posting wasn't necessarily obvious and he hoped no one would be able to find him simply because he got online. Even so, he responded to a few posts, making it clear that he appreciated the compliments and was delighted to hear people were enjoying the new book as well as his older ones.

Another best seller? He certainly hoped so. It already seemed to be heading that way.

By the time he felt he'd done enough, it was definitely quite late. And he wanted to get up reasonably early to go to breakfast when most of the others would be in the cafeteria.

Especially Janna.

He'd shower in the morning, so now he just got ready to lie down in the small but hopefully comfortable bed.

He wished he could contact Janna then, but he had no way to call her. He would have even had a good excuse: to talk to her about what he'd read so far in her manuscript.

He could do that in the morning. He'd take her aside at breakfast, or maybe afterward before they both got too busy.

As he pondered Janna's story and her writing—and her—he fell asleep.

Chapter 5

"Wizzy, come," Janna called. She'd gotten up only a short while ago, showered and dressed in a Chance Animal Shelter shirt and nice slacks. She would put on fresh vet tech scrubs later at the clinic. Now it was time to take her wonderful Australian shepherd mix for his morning outing. He hadn't indicated he was in a hurry, but she didn't want him to wait any longer. She would feed him once they got to the clinic.

He'd been hanging out in the short hallway, following her from bedroom to bathroom and back, then lying down and watching her. Now, he quickly obeyed her command.

Soon, they were walking down the flight of steps to the ground floor, saying hi to a few of the staffers who were going toward the cafeteria for breakfast. Janna would eventually as well, but first she wanted to check on the animals in her care. Hopefully all were doing well.

Janna couldn't help glancing back up the stairs, and then over toward the elevators. No sign of Josh yet.

Was he already inside the cafeteria? Had he read any of her manuscript? Nolan Hoffsler or not, she was eager to hear his opinion. Was he actually who she believed he was?

Okay, enough wondering about that. Maybe she would find out, and maybe she wouldn't. Either way, she was eager to hear someone else's view of what she had written. Even if Josh wasn't the best-selling mystery author, she could tell he was a smart guy, and he'd indicated he at least liked to read. She couldn't necessarily rely on anything he said, but still...

And she definitely couldn't allow her attraction to him to go any farther than it already had. In fact, she needed to erase it from her mind.

She snapped on Wizzy's leash, and they went outside. He might be okay wandering around here, but she was more comfortable keeping him close this way, at least for now. She began leading him along the path between the buildings where the animals were housed, going slowly enough for him to sniff and do what he wanted.

"Good morning," said a female voice from behind her. Janna turned to see Nella walking toward her alone. "Everything okay?" the assistant director asked.

"Definitely, so far at least," Janna answered. "Once Wizzy's ready, we'll head to the clinic to make sure all's well."

"I figured," Nella said. "I'm just going to peek into each of the animal buildings to make sure everyone's okay before heading to breakfast."

"Let me know if you see anything wrong." Vet tech Janna was always prepared for whatever an animal might need at the shelter, as well as at the clinic she worked for in downtown Chance.

"Definitely." Nella held up her hand in a wave and continued walking briskly down the path.

By then Wizzy had taken care of what he generally needed to, and Janna cleaned up after him. Then they headed on toward the clinic. She didn't meet many staff members coming from this direction toward breakfast, but she'd join at least some of them in the cafeteria later.

Including Josh?

Really, enough, she told herself again. She let herself into the vet clinic with her key.

First, she put Wizzy in his usual enclosure where he stayed when he wasn't outside playing with staff members. After she fed him, she headed for Squeegee's enclosure in the front, away from the other dogs. The pup must have heard her—he was sitting up and wagging his tail. His sore paw was on the ground, although she couldn't tell if he placed any pressure on it.

"Hi, guy," she said to the chocolate Lab mix before opening the gate.

Squeegee immediately came out and sat in front of her. This time, he raised his paw but just a little.

Did it feel better? Janna hoped so. She knelt on the floor, putting her hand out to take Squeegee's paw and hold it gently. He didn't wince or try to pull it away, both good signs. "Let's go into the exam room so I can take a look at it," she told him. When she rose, he started following her, and she watched his limp—not nearly as bad as it had been the previous day.

Was he actually healing?

She smiled slightly as she picked up Squeegee and put him on the table in the exam room, this time without

Josh's help. That was her norm, but she kind of wished he was here to assist her. Which was silly.

But before she could take the bandage off Squeegee's paw, she heard a knock at the clinic's front door. Who could that be? Dr. Kornel was due here today and could arrive any time, but he had his own key card.

"Okay, boy. Let's put you back down for now." Janna lifted Squeegee again and set him on the floor. "Stay," she said, pointing toward him. She didn't know how many commands he recognized, but she knew that the staff here worked with the dogs, teaching them obedience, and *stay* was a common command.

He obeyed, at least, as she left him in the exam room and went to the front door. "Who's there?" she called.

"Oh, good, you are here," said a familiar deep voice. "It's Josh."

She opened the door. Yes, it was the tall, muscular man she was supposed to call Josh standing there, in—what else?—a Chance Animal Shelter T-shirt, a brown one today. He smiled as he regarded her with eyes that were an even deeper brown than his shirt. His thick, dark hair seemed a little damp, and she assumed he'd recently showered.

"Hi," she said. "Come on in." But why was he here rather than at breakfast?

He answered her unspoken question right away. "I thought you might be here when I peeked into the cafeteria and didn't see you. Is it okay if I hang out with you while you look in on the animals?"

"Sure," she said. But had he read her manuscript? Was

he going to mention it? She had to assume that was why he was really here.

And once more he answered her thoughts. "I did read part of your manuscript," he said. "I don't imagine this is a good time to talk about it, while you're checking on the animals, right? And then you'll want to have breakfast. But hopefully we can hang out a little while after that, if you've got some time you can spare away from the clinic. I'm eager to talk to you about it."

Uh-oh. That couldn't be good.

Her expression, as she aimed a half smile at him, must have given away her thoughts. "You look worried," he said with a brief laugh. "Don't be. Not that I'm an expert—"

Yeah, right, she thought.

"But I really liked it. I have some thoughts and suggestions I can convey to you. But I think you're off to a great start."

Janna felt herself take a deep breath and realized she'd been holding it. But she felt relieved that the first person who'd at least started reading her story wasn't immediately bashing it. And if he just happened to be—

"Anyway, why don't I watch while you examine the animals, then we can head to breakfast together?"

"Sounds good. I was just about to examine Squeegee's paw."

"I'll lift him on to the table for you."

Janna resisted laughing. "I appreciate that." She turned toward the exam room. "Please come this way."

And she noted happily that this sexy, good-looking man obeyed her.

Could she get him to obey her in other ways?

She managed to prevent herself from laughing out loud at that thought too.

In the exam room, Squeegee stood from where he'd been lying on the tile floor below the table.

"Hi, guy," Janna greeted him again.

"Yeah, hi," Josh said. "How are you doing?"

The pup's tail wagged, and Janna was happy to see that. Maybe he was doing a lot better. She was eager to check his paw.

She felt even more eager to get close to Josh as he bent to pick the dog up and place him gently on the table.

"Thanks," she said. "Squeegee thanks you too. Josh, would you please put your hand on his back to keep him in place as I take his bandage off?"

"Sure."

She leaned close, placing her shoulder briefly against his.

Why did that feel so good?

No matter. She moved to face Squeegee on the table and carefully began to remove the bandage. The dog's paw definitely appeared to be healing. Sure, there was still a certain rawness to it, and she would need to treat it with an antiseptic again. But it had improved.

"What do you think?" Josh asked. He was standing near her, peering over her shoulder, but not too close to make her examination difficult.

She gathered he cared. She appreciated that.

"Better than yesterday," she said. "It seems to be improving, slowly but definitely. I'm happy with how he's coming along. And I'll be pleased to show the veterinarian, not just a vet tech like me, when he arrives later."

"Don't sell yourself short," Josh said. Had he drawn even closer to talk into her ear? But then he backed away. "You obviously know what you're doing. At least Squeegee must think so."

At the sound of his name, the dog, who'd had his head lowered while Janna worked with him, looked up and seemed to meet Josh's eyes.

Janna laughed. "Maybe he does. And I think I do know what I'm doing. So let me do my thing and medicate that sore spot again and rebandage it. Then I'll go check on the other animals—and yes, you're welcome to join me."

After Janna treated and bandaged his paw again, Squeegee seemed just fine when Josh helped the pup back down to the floor. Janna put him into his enclosure, then went to check on Pekie and Elmer and Furball with Josh's company. Fortunately, they all seemed okay too, and Janna suspected that Dr. Kornel would have them all returned to their normal locations in the shelter when he got there that day.

When she was done, Josh said, "Hey, I'm hungry. You ready for breakfast?"

"Definitely," she said. Together, they gathered Wizzy from his enclosure. Josh stooped to pet him, and Wizzy wagged his tail. Then they all headed from the clinic toward the cafeteria.

Janna was hungry now. And she felt sure she would continue to enjoy the company.

* * *

That had gone well, Josh thought. He enjoyed being in Janna's company, and watching her care for the animals helped calm his thoughts, at least a bit. For now.

Before he left his apartment that morning, he'd made the mistake of checking his emails once more. There was one from a source he recognized—the person who'd been threatening him. The username was different, so he realized only after he opened it and saw the latest threats that the email address was familiar to him, even if the name wasn't.

Whoever it was had been clever enough to keep his—or her—IP address and location untraceable. Oh, the cops and even the investigators he'd hired before were able to discern that the stalker's location might be somewhere around where he lived in San Diego. But just the general area, no specifics. Nothing that could really help determine who the person was. Josh wasn't especially technologically inclined, but even those experts he spoke with seemed stymied.

Fortunately, whoever it was sounded angry and frustrated and even more threatening today—because they were also unable to determine Josh's location. His stalker sounded angry that the murder victim in his latest book seemed based on a real victim: Jaxon Draybell. Nolan was obviously out somewhere in hiding and needed to go home fast, they said, or there would be some bad repercussions.

Then there were some general threats against Nolan Hoffsler on a couple social media sites, again from an unknown source.

Josh would talk to Scott about the situation later, even though he felt fairly safe now, hidden and protected at Chance Animal Shelter. He had no desire to leave here soon.

In fact, hanging out with someone he'd already come to like—a lot—seemed highly preferable.

It didn't take long for Josh and Janna to reach the cafeteria. The place was crowded enough that they had to hunt around for a few minutes for available seats. But everyone knew vet tech Janna, and she'd soon been invited, with Wizzy, to join a few staffers, some of whom Josh had already met, including Chessie, a young woman who seemed to know everyone, and Augie, an older guy who also seemed friendly. Janna asked Chessie to hold Wizzy's leash while she and Josh got their food, and together they started for the cafeteria line.

But when Josh saw Scott enter the room along with Nella, he changed direction and headed toward the director. Josh shot Janna a smile at her quizzical look. This might not be the best time to talk to Scott, but he at least wanted to let him know he had something to discuss sometime that morning.

Scott's gaze immediately focused on him. "Hey, Josh," he said. "Good morning. Are you having fun here yet?" He smiled broadly, but his look was questioning.

"Definitely fun here," Josh responded, then drew slightly closer. "But there's something I need to talk to you about." He wasn't going to mention here that he'd received a new threatening email. Not while other staff members might hear him. He was one of the very few staffers permitted to communicate at all with the outside world, even if it was only by email. And fortunately it seemed as if his enemy still hadn't found him.

But Josh couldn't help focusing on the frustration apparent in the email that mentioned Jaxon's name—and promised that Nolan's fate would be similar...

No use thinking about that now, when he couldn't even talk to anyone about it, let alone find the menace and stop them.

"You okay?" Scott was staring at him, concern written all over his face.

Again, this wasn't the time. "Just hungry," Josh said and smiled. "Ah, it looks like Janna is getting her meal. I was with her at the vet clinic this morning when she checked on the animals, and we decided to have breakfast together. I'll join her now. But I hope you and I can talk soon."

"Okay," Scott said. "And I do have a meeting right after breakfast. How about if you come to my office around ten this morning?"

"Sounds good," Josh said, feeling a little frustrated they couldn't meet earlier. Still, that might give him time to talk with Janna about her story. And her presence seemed to calm him, since he concentrated more on her than all the other things on his mind.

Like the threats against him...

For now, he waited in the serving line with Janna and soon was able to put some scrambled eggs, fried potatoes and toast on a plate. He certainly wasn't starving, but he'd be able to eat and enjoy a breakfast like this. He got a cup of coffee, then watched Scott head to his usual table.

Josh went to join Janna at the seats they'd picked out earlier.

"How's your meal?" he asked as he sat down, with Augie on his other side. Chessie was across from them, and he'd met the people who sat on either side of her, too—bald, middle-aged Jerry, and Veronica, who looked similar in age to Jerry.

"Delightful as always," Janna said, "especially considering the company." She aimed a smile at him, then also looked across the table. Her companions grinned back.

Josh noticed that Wizzy lay under the table, with Janna holding his leash. "Hi, guy," Josh said as the dog met his eyes, and Wizzy's tail started wagging. Josh looked at Janna. "Is it okay if I give him a piece of toast?"

"Sure," she said. "A small one. I'll give him some eggs shortly."

The conversation at the table was friendly, mostly discussing some of the dogs the staff members had been training. Josh wanted to join them and make himself useful here at the shelter. Later.

But for now, he quietly asked Janna, "Do you have time to talk after breakfast?" He figured she would know why—to go over his thoughts about her manuscript. And it would be nice to spend some time with her till he was able to visit with Scott.

"Probably," she said, looking at him with her lovely green eyes. "But first I need to return to the clinic since Dr. Kornel should be there."

"If it's okay, I'll go with you. Then we can see if there'll be time for us to talk later."

She nodded, and a smile lit her pretty face. "Sounds

good. And you can walk with me when I look in on the animals again—probably."

And afterward, if he couldn't yet meet with Scott, Josh could at least go walk a dog or two outside along with other staff members, even work on some training.

Not that any of that would really keep his mind off his issues, but at least he wouldn't have to dwell on them now.

He hoped.

Chapter 6

Janna felt she'd had a good breakfast, both because of the food and the company. She was glad she wasn't in a position to need to become a staff member at Chance Animal Shelter, but she appreciated meeting and hanging out with the people when she wasn't taking care of the animals. Even though she had nothing to do with the staff members' protection.

"Do you know if the vet you're working with will be there when we arrive?" Josh asked.

He, Janna and Wizzy were on their way to the clinic. He held Wizzy's leash and stopped now and then to give her dog a command or two, as well as a treat—a small portion of toast, which Janna had already approved.

"I don't know for sure, but it's almost eight thirty," Janna responded. "That's when Dr. Kornel often shows up. Since he hasn't called to say he'll be late, I figure he's either there already or will be soon."

Why did Josh care? Was he just attempting to make conversation? That made some sense, since this wouldn't be a good time to talk about her manuscript. And they'd already looked in on the animals under her care, so that wasn't something they necessarily needed to talk about either.

He might not appreciate her asking again about who he was or what he was doing there—as she'd done more than once since they had met yesterday.

And she'd gotten the sense when they visited the clinic earlier, and again when he'd gone up to Scott in the cafeteria, that something was on Josh's mind. Something was stressing him out.

Something he probably also didn't want to talk about with her.

They reached the clinic, and Janna used her key card to open it. She heard some light noise, probably from one of the enclosures, though she couldn't tell if it was where the dogs were or Furball the cat.

"Sounds like the vet is here, right?" Josh asked, his voice low as if he figured he might not be welcome. Well, Janna would make sure Kyle would accept his presence as an observer, or at least she would try.

"I think so. Let's see if Dr. Kornel is examining Squeegee."

She led Wizzy into one of the empty enclosures and, petting him first, shut him behind the wire gate. "Stay, Wiz," she said. "Good boy." She put on a fresh scrubs jacket now that she was officially on duty. She had several but would need to run them through the clinic's washing machine soon.

Josh had waited for her, although he was looking down the hall toward where the low noise seemed to come from. Janna gestured for him to follow, and they headed that way.

Sure enough, Kyle was in an exam room with Squeegee, the door open. The dog sat on the table with the bandage removed from his sore paw. Kyle obviously heard Janna's arrival, turning toward them slightly.

Janna's boss was a tall guy with short black hair, and like her he'd already donned his blue scrubs. "Good morning," he told her. Nodding slightly to Squeegee, he added, "And good job. Looks like this guy is healing nicely, just as you told me."

Janna felt herself relax slightly. She knew she'd done a good job and had also felt happy about Squeegee's improvement, but it helped to have Kyle agree and recognize the positive change.

"Thanks," she said. "I couldn't be happier that Squeegee is doing better."

She saw Kyle's gaze shift over her shoulder. "And hi to you," the vet said. "Are you a new staff member here?"

It was a logical assumption, considering that Josh wore a Chance Animal Shelter T-shirt. But then, managers here did sometimes too.

"Yes," Josh said. "I'm Josh Forlett, and I just arrived here yesterday."

"I know better than to ask you why," the vet said. "But I can say you're welcome here, Josh. I assume you like animals or you wouldn't have been accepted at the shelter—and I can make that assumption even more since you're visiting this clinic." But Kyle did aim a quick grin at Janna, as if he was making additional assumptions—like maybe Josh was here at the clinic just as much because of her.

Which might be true, since they'd been hanging out

together more than was appropriate. But Janna wasn't about to tell her boss that she'd been trying to get this man's opinion of her writing, let alone tell him why that might really matter.

"Yes," Josh said. "I definitely like animals. And first met vet tech Janna when she was going after Squeegee, who dashed—er, limped—out of here when he should have stayed inside the clinic."

"Well, thanks for helping out," the vet said.

A sudden idea came to Janna. "Have you looked in on Pekie and Elmer yet? I think both have pretty well healed from their minor injuries, and I was thinking about taking them for a walk—maybe with Josh's help. If they're doing as well as I believe, maybe they can be returned to their usual areas in the shelter and go back to being trained by the staff members?"

"No, I haven't checked them yet," Kyle said, "but let's go do it. I'll be really glad if they're doing that well. How do you feel about walking one of them, Josh?"

"Sounds good to me," he replied, which made Janna happy. They'd be alone together for a while, though not really alone. Still, maybe they'd be able to talk.

Janna helped Kyle put an antiseptic on Squeegee's sore spot, then bandage his paw again. Kyle gently returned the dog to his enclosure, then went to check on the other two dogs, with Janna and Josh following.

The vet stopped and smiled at how both dogs were sitting up behind the metal mesh of their enclosures, wagging their tails. "Hi, guys," Kyle said. "Let's take a look at you."

The vet put each dog onto the examination table and

checked them out, opening their mouths and looking at their tongues and teeth, gently squeezing their bodies and examining their hind ends. Neither had had obvious injuries like Squeegee, but they'd both been listless. Kyle had done bloodwork on both, but there'd been no indication of infection. It wasn't clear why they'd been acting that way, but fortunately they were the only dogs at the shelter who were, so they apparently didn't have something contagious.

Kyle leashed each of them and had them walk beside him briefly. Nothing looked bad—definitely a good thing.

"Okay," the vet finally said. "Go ahead and take them for a walk together. If they seem fine, you can take them to their appropriate buildings and have staff members find them enclosures there. It'll be fine to start their training again. Right now, I'm going to look in on Furball. If she's doing as well as these pups, I'll take her to the cat building myself. She won't be going on a walk with you or me or anyone, after all."

Janna laughed. "No, that wouldn't be a good idea. But I certainly hope she's as well as these guys are."

Kyle left the exam room, and Janna turned to Josh. "Are you ready to take a walk?" She definitely hoped he was. And that he was also ready to talk.

"Sure," he said. "Let's do it."

"Wait here a minute," Janna said. She hurried to one of the storerooms where they kept leashes and picked up a couple, then brought them back and handed one to Josh. "How about if I walk Pekie and you walk Elmer?"

She figured a strong guy like Josh would prefer handling a retriever mix over a Pekingese.

"Hey, I like little dogs," Josh said, giving her a frown—that quickly turned into a smile. "Bigger dogs too. And I think Elmer and I will get along fine."

Janna smiled back. She put the leash on Pekie, and Josh did the same with Elmer. They went outside and started walking the dogs in the courtyard.

They weren't alone. Several staff members were also walking dogs, but they seemed to be hanging out together, which was a good thing. One of the managers, Telma, was out there too. Their being in one area allowed Janna to lead Josh and the dogs they were walking in a direction no one else appeared to be at the moment.

"So how's Elmer treating you?" she asked Josh. The retriever was sniffing the ground a lot, mostly the lawn beside the paved path, but, heck, he was a dog, and retrievers had particularly good senses of scent.

"I'm wondering what smells so good down there, but I'm not about to bend down to find out."

"I figured," Janna said. She waited for a couple of minutes while both dogs sniffed. Finally they walked on with the humans accompanying them. And then she asked what she'd wanted to all along. "Can we talk about what part of my manuscript you read and specifics about what you liked and didn't like and why?"

Josh laughed. "Gee, why am I not surprised you want to talk about that now?"

"Well, I'm just not sure when, if ever, we'll really get to hang out alone in one of our apartments or otherwise to discuss it, and you know I'm eager to hear… Nolan."

She was glad that he laughed rather than objecting or getting irritated at her. In fact...

He stopped walking and looked down at her with those brown eyes of his looking serious—and sexy. "Okay, Janna," he said. "Can you promise to keep a secret?"

She knew what that secret was even before he admitted anything. But she also knew she couldn't let anyone else know. "Absolutely," she told him, staring straight back at him while the dogs maneuvered between their legs.

"Well, I am who you think I am. And this isn't really the time or place for me to give you my specific thoughts about your manuscript, not without having it with us. I think it's good, but it does need some work. We'll have to figure out when we can really talk about it."

She felt her breath whoosh out of her as her grin broadened. "Got it, Josh. I'll look forward to it, whenever that might be."

"Okay, let's just continue our walk for now. We'll figure something out."

"Absolutely."

But as thrilled as she was, the other thing that had been grating at her rushed to the surface, and she couldn't help stopping once more, looking up at him and blurting, "But why are you really here? Has someone really threatened you?"

"Yes, damn it," he said, gritting his teeth as he looked back at her. "And they're at it again."

He knew he shouldn't have said anything. Shouldn't continue to say anything. But Josh knew he had Janna's attention, and she seemed to give a damn.

Not that she—or most likely anyone else here—could do anything about it. Not even when he got to speak with Scott later.

But it might help his state of mind to talk to someone right now. And he did trust Janna. She wouldn't tell anyone. And the sympathy she was likely to show just might help him feel a little better.

For now, though, he just bent a little and gave Elmer a slight pat on the head. The retriever sat and looked up at him as if in thanks. And caring.

Oh, heck. He was reading too much into that—maybe because he needed to feel that at least someone gave a damn about him at the moment. And if it was a dog, that was fine.

But he also had a person with him. A person who wanted to talk to him—who'd known who he was from the beginning.

"You okay?" she asked.

Josh removed his gaze from Elmer and looked straight into Janna's lovely face. Into those eyes that regarded him with such concern.

"Yeah," he said. "Let's walk."

"Definitely. Although I do need to return to the clinic to work soon. Even though Dr. Kornel encouraged this walk, he'll need to finish his review of the animals there today, then we'll both head to our downtown clinic."

"Got it," Josh said. That was a good thing. Sure, he was in a mood to talk, and he'd tell her some of what was in his head, but that couldn't go on for long.

Especially since he was hoping he'd get to really hash out the contents of his latest threats with Scott soon.

They started down the path toward the building where cats and other animals who weren't dogs were housed. The other staff members who were out—and there were quite a few of them—were mostly going the other direction, sometimes hanging out together and talking. Or stopping to give the dogs under their care a command or two. The training for the dogs here had clearly been productive, since there were a lot of sits, stays, downs and comes that seemed to be obeyed.

But for the moment, Janna and he remained quiet. Until—

"Okay," she said as they passed the small dog building. "I don't think anyone can hear us. But…well, I gather there's something wrong. You don't have to talk about it. In fact, a real writer like you might be better off just writing about it. Getting something written down and dealt with even fictionally could make you feel better. For me, though—even though I like writing, I've found that talking about difficult things with someone who's really listening sometimes helps. And you can be sure I'll really listen."

Josh didn't mean to laugh, but he did. Not that it was a genuine laugh of amusement, but more of wryness. "Okay. I'm sure you know better than to repeat anything I tell you. And I'm hoping to discuss it with Scott a little later today. But talking about it now might improve my state of mind." He hoped. And he hoped trusting the woman walking with him wouldn't be a mistake.

But expressing what was on his mind—and not just on his computer screen—might actually help him deal with it better.

"I'll do all I can," Janna said, then stopped. Pekie had squatted along the walkway, and Janna waited while the little dog did her thing—nothing that required any cleanup, at least. "As soon as I can," Janna added.

This time Josh actually found himself laughing, though not for long. But he did feel amused with his company and what was going on. And that did help his state of mind, at least a little.

"Okay," Janna said when they began walking again. "Are you ready to talk? Or—well, if it would just make things worse to keep whatever it is at the front of your mind to tell me about it, then—"

He stopped walking for just a moment and looked down at Janna, who glanced up at him. "No, I definitely need to talk about it, though it makes more sense for me to burden Scott with it than you. But he's not available till later. So, yes, this is something I can and will write about, especially since I do write a lot about nasty things happening to people. Suspense and threats and murders… But you know that, since you said you've read some of my stuff."

"I have." Janna's voice sounded somewhat gravelly, and then she cleared her throat as they continued walking. "Are you telling me indirectly that there's something actually going on in your life—suspense and threats and murders? I figured there might be, since you're here."

"Yes to the suspense and threats," he said. "And though there was an actual murder that occurred near me similar to the one I described in my most recent book, what's really driving me nuts are the threats against me. Threats that I'll be murdered soon."

"What!" Janna exclaimed, and she stopped walking, which caused both dogs to also stop and sit down and look up at the humans.

"Yeah," Josh said. "What sent me here and got me to apply to become a staff member was that someone has been threatening me. Badly. And now, I'm being threatened online on social media sites and email, telling me I need to let the world know where I am."

"Which would be nuts!" Janna said. "Especially if that murderer is looking for you."

"Yep. And I'm not so gullible."

"Who do you think it is?" Janna demanded. Pekie pulled a little on her leash but soon stopped.

"If I knew, I wouldn't be here," he said. "The cops on the case couldn't figure it out either, and I even hired a private detective firm to help out. The threats started after my latest book was published, so I wondered if I might have said something in it that triggered the stalker. The novel is based loosely on a real murder that occurred in a restaurant near where I live, partly since I didn't believe the suspect brought in, then released, was the real killer anyway. But I didn't—couldn't—point to anyone else either. I was just hoping the authorities would keep looking into it despite my making up a fictional killer."

"Which does sound like a reason the real guilty party might get worried, and angry."

"Maybe."

Janna asked a few more questions about the murder that was the basis of his story. She'd obviously read the book, which made him glad. And it did help somewhat for him to talk about not only what had brought him here, but the situation that continued to eat at his mind as it got worse.

They'd been walking Elmer and Pekie for about ten minutes now, and Josh was enjoying Janna's company—and her apparent compassion about what had brought him here and how he felt about it. She asked questions that indicated she cared and was willing to listen if he wanted to talk more about it and give her thoughts—although she was a vet tech and not a detective.

On the other hand, the manuscript she'd given him to look at made it clear she enjoyed writing mysteries and suspense, and even researching situations like the one he'd gotten himself into. Plus, she'd read his stories and probably others in the genre, so she was a mystery fan.

But she wasn't going to be able to figure out who was threatening him any more than he could—not here. And he wasn't about to leave now that he'd been accepted at Chance, at least not for a while. Not till he figured out how to get the authorities to find out who was menacing him, apparently at least partially out of the person's frustration that he seemed to have disappeared.

Still, he wasn't surprised when Janna stopped walking, told Pekie to sit and looked at Josh, who did the same with Elmer.

"Sorry," she said. "But I need to go back to the clinic and help Dr. Kornel finish up here at the shelter for the day. It'll soon be time to head to downtown Chance, to the clinic there for the afternoon."

"Got it," he said. Her leaving might even be a good thing, since he'd possibly be able to find a way to ap-

propriately nag Scott to see him and discuss the current situation faster. Or not. But it wouldn't hurt to try.

"Good. Let's go back now." She seemed to hesitate.
"But, well, maybe we can get together soon to discuss
your actual suspects, who may be threatening you. And
also discuss my manuscript a bit, if there's time." They
had turned and were walking in the slightly cool air of
the September morning back toward the main buildings
that held the clinic and cafeteria—and Scott's office.
That was fine with Josh.

The idea of seeing Janna again soon, and somehow
getting alone with her and not just out here where there
were a lot of other staff members around, sounded much
better than it should have. Maybe it just felt good, now
that he had to be on his own and not with his usual
friends, to try to make sure he survived.

"I'd be very happy to figure out some alone time with
you." Oh, that sounded too suggestive—and he really
shouldn't allow himself to feel so attracted to this woman,
for many reasons—so he continued, "I really want to
talk to you about your manuscript and writing and all.
And yes, talking about my situation sounds good too.
But you said you're going to the veterinary clinic downtown, right?"

"Yes, and I probably won't be back here today since
none of the animals need extra care. But I'll be back tomorrow, and maybe we can figure something out then."

"Sounds good to me."

They walked the dogs back to the clinic and gave
them some treats. Kyle was in the front room with

Squeegee. "This pup is still doing pretty well. How about those two?"

"Both seemed fine," Janna told him.

"Great. Why don't you and I confirm with Scott or Nella that it's okay, then get all of them restored to the main shelter by staff members? We'll both be here again tomorrow so we can check on them, and of course I'll make it clear I'm to be called if anything seems wrong—including with Furball."

Josh figured there was no reason for him to hang out here any longer, so he said goodbye to both of them. He'd look forward to seeing Janna tomorrow, assuming that all worked out.

She smiled at him but didn't say anything else—except with her lovely eyes. She appeared concerned, and he wasn't sure whether that was because she still recognized his state of mind, or she cared whether they'd get together tomorrow, or both.

Didn't matter. And he ignored his sudden urge to give her a hug before he left. Absurd!

Quietly, he headed toward the offices. It was still early to talk to Scott, but still… Josh entered the office building, went up to the fourth floor and walked to the last door, half expecting there would be no answer to his knock.

Instead, Scott opened the door. "Hey," he said, "good timing. I was just about to go try to find you."

Josh felt a little flicker of relief inside, both because he was going to get to talk to Scott now, and because the shelter director clearly wasn't annoyed with him for showing up. He followed Scott inside.

Their conversation was brief, with Scott sitting beside Josh on one of the chairs facing his desk. Josh got into his email on Scott's computer and showed him the latest threatening emails. "Jaxon Draybell is the name of the murder victim I based my latest book on, the restaurant owner." And then he pointed out the bottom line of the messages: if Nolan didn't show up at home, he'd be found soon anyway—and his fate would be similar.

The social media hints weren't as clear but seemed to be more like fans wondering where he was and if he was making any appearances. A few were pushier, though.

"I don't believe that whoever it is knows where I am," Josh said, "especially since they sound frustrated they can't find me. But these are some of the most specific threats I've gotten, after the initial attacks of that fire and gunshot. Although they must assume I'm an idiot, if they think I'd suddenly reappear because they told me to, so they could kill me."

Scott's laugh was short and wry. "That's for sure. Well, you shouldn't respond or contact anyone from before you came here. But I'll make sure the authorities in your home area are aware of the latest threats you've received. Thanks for letting me know." "And thank you for helping me," Josh added.

He soon left, heading for the areas where staffers walked and trained dogs.

Nervous or not, he was a staffer here now and would stay that way for a while. Hopefully safely.

And for now, he'd also look forward to seeing vet tech Janna. To talk to her about her manuscript, of course. And maybe more. Right now, she was just someone else in his new, hopefully short, stint here at this place till he felt safe again.

But it didn't hurt to have something, or someone, to look forward to.

Chapter 7

Wow. Talking with Josh—no, Nolan—made Janna wish she had more skills in solving mysteries and saving people than just in the story she was writing. She'd suspected he was here because of a problem. She didn't know him well, but she trusted him already and didn't believe he'd come just to check out the shelter and use it in a book. No, a problem of his own had brought him here. Something nasty, from what he'd so briefly described. Scary.

Janna knew that even as she returned to work, Josh's story would be gnawing at her mind.

The morning was growing later. Janna got her wonderful Wizzy out of his enclosure and took him for a quick walk, then gave him some treats and brought him back to a large fenced-in area inside for a while as she finished up at the clinic. He couldn't exactly get a lot of exercise there, but he'd have more room to move around.

Giving her pup a big hug, she promised him, "See you soon."

She hurried to Kyle's office. He was sitting at his desk, going over medical charts. "All looks good here," he told her, "but I've been waiting for you before I tell

Scott to come by and have our patients taken back to where they belong. Including Squeegee. I think he's doing well enough to leave the clinic, but we'll need to tell Scott to be sure he's observed a lot."

"Sounds good," Janna said, and it really did. That meant Kyle agreed that the four animals they'd been taking care of here had improved as much as she believed. Even though what had brought them here wasn't always clear, they were getting back to their best once more. She knew that was so with Pekie and Elmer, especially after the latest walk.

The walk they'd taken with Josh...

No, this wasn't the time to think about him.

At the moment, she helped Kyle do a quick exam of Furball, who purred and meowed and acted just as a healthy kitty should. Yes!

They returned to Pekie and Elmer, where both dogs stood behind the mesh gates of their enclosures and pawed at them, wagging their tails. Nothing to indicate they felt anything but good, no matter how they'd been the last couple of days. Yes again!

And Squeegee? He was putting some weight on his sore paw. He would definitely need to be observed, but he seemed to be doing well.

"Okay, then," Kyle said. "Let's call Scott."

Before joining him in his office, Janna removed Wizzy from his enclosure, and her wonderful pup jumped on her as if wanting to hug her. She hugged him back. "You're such a good boy for being so patient with me," she told him. "But you know that."

Wizzy was definitely a smart boy too. He might not

understand her words, but she was fairly certain he understood the loving emotion she intended to convey.

She leashed him as usual, even though he was smart and well-behaved enough to remain by her side. But though he sometimes ran around in the open area inside the shelter, this wasn't the time for it.

Kyle was sitting behind his desk when Janna and Wizzy entered his office.

"Hi, Wizzy," he said without rising, and Wizzy wagged his tail again. "Ready for our call?" he asked Janna.

"Sure."

As he picked up his cell phone, Janna couldn't help wondering if Josh might be in the shelter director's office now. He'd indicated he meant to talk with Scott about what was happening with him that morning, but it was now afternoon.

But Scott answered right away. Kyle had him on speaker. "Everything okay?" he asked.

"Definitely," Kyle said, and he described how well all the animals now in the clinic were doing, including Squeegee.

"Really glad to hear that," the director said. "I'll come there in a few minutes with Nella, and we'll take them back to their places in the shelter. And yes, we'll get the staff members to check especially on Squeegee to be sure he doesn't appear to be getting worse again."

"Sounds good," Kyle said. He looked at Janna. "Unfortunately, I need to leave right away, but Janna will be here when you come by. Okay, Janna?"

"Sure," she said. He was her boss, after all, and if he wanted her to hang out here a little longer, that was fine.

She enjoyed working at this clinic, just as she did the one downtown. They fortunately weren't usually very busy here, since the animals at the shelter were well taken care of. The staff members watching over and training them really seemed to give a damn.

Would she see Josh again today before she left? Unlikely, and even if she did they probably wouldn't be able to talk again. But she'd be back—and sometime, tomorrow or otherwise, she'd find a way to get him alone for a while so he could talk to her about her manuscript.

Sometime. That was the key.

Oh, well. She was a veterinary technician who hoped to be a writer on the side. And here, as well as at the downtown clinic, she would be caring for animals who needed medical care. That was what was important.

"Okay, one more check on our patients," Kyle said. "Then I'm out of here."

So that was what they did after Janna returned Wizzy to his enclosure. No change in the other animals here, which wasn't surprising considering the care and examinations they'd been given earlier.

Kyle briefly returned to his office, medical bag in his hand. "I'll see you later downtown," he said.

Only, a knock sounded on the door. That wouldn't be Scott or Nella. They each had keys to get in. Who was it, then?

Kyle reached the door and opened it. Janna couldn't see at first who it was, but Kyle stepped back. "Come in. What's wrong with her?"

Her who? But Janna saw immediately that Josh was carrying Mika, an adorable beagle mix who'd been brought into the shelter just a couple of weeks ago after her owner dumped her when moving away from Chance. It had been such a shame, but everyone at Chance Animal Shelter was taking good, loving care of her.

Only—

"Mika was playing with a couple of the other dogs near one end of the walkway when she tried running too fast, I guess," Josh said. "I saw it happen, though I was working with one of the other dogs. But poor Mika somehow fell sideways off the pavement, and when she tried to get up she was obviously in pain. I told the others I'd bring her here, since I knew you were still here. Or at least I hoped you were."

He glanced toward Janna, but she looked directly at Kyle. "You came at a good time, fortunately," she said. "Dr. Kornel was just about to leave to go to the clinic downtown."

"Glad I caught you, then," Josh said. His smile was dim and questioning, as if he wondered whether Kyle would stay to look at Mika's problem.

"Me too," Kyle said. "Bring Mika into the examination room."

Fortunately, the pup, as a beagle mix, wasn't too large. But Janna was sure that Josh was strong enough to pick up nearly any size dog and carry it here to the clinic.

Mika soon was on the examination table with Kyle looking over her. "She's got a scrape on her side," the vet said. "But not very large, or deep. It doesn't look too serious. I think I can get on my way since I'm already running late, but, Janna, I want you to shave the area, clean and sterilize it, then bandage it."

She was used to doing such things. But she did pay close attention while Kyle pointed out the problem. It wasn't extremely large and didn't look too bad, but she imagined poor Mika was still hurting since scrapes like that could really sting. "I assume I can give her a pain reliever too," she told Kyle, who agreed immediately.

"I don't think you'll need much help keeping Mika on the table while you work," Kyle said, "but Josh—" He looked at the other man. "Would you mind hanging around just in case Janna needs you to hold Mika in place?"

"I'd be glad to help," Josh said, glancing first at the dog, then at Janna. She felt he was talking to her, and it made her feel all squishy inside. Which was ridiculous.

"See you at the downtown clinic later, Janna," Kyle said. "And, Josh, thanks for helping."

Kyle left the examination room. As Janna gathered supplies to help clean and care for Mika's wound, she heard the clinic door open and shut.

Asking Josh to hold Mika firmly so she couldn't move, Janna used a battery-operated razor to remove the hair around the wound. Then she used an antiseptic to clean the wound and added a bit of pain reliever. Fortunately, because of its relatively small size she was able to cover it with just one adhesive pad that she attached with a tape that wouldn't hurt a dog if it was chewed. Even so, the wound was at a location on Mika's side that the beagle couldn't easily reach.

When Janna was done, she put what was called familiarly a "cone of shame" over the poor pup's head. The plastic recovery cone would make it even more difficult for Mika to lick the wound. She also gave her a bit of sedative to make sure she stayed calm.

As she finished, Janna heard the clinic door open, and Scott came in with Nella, both in their Chance Animal Shelter shirts—with concerned expressions on their faces. "I heard from a couple of the staffers that Mika got hurt." Scott looked past Janna to where Josh still held Mika on the exam table.

"Yes, but fortunately it's not bad." Janna described it to the director since he couldn't see the bandaged injury. "I've given her a slight sedative, so she'll soon be sleeping for a while. I need to head downtown now but of course will return tomorrow. So will Dr. Kornel, and we should be able to remove the cone then if all goes well. Although if she starts looking bad just call me and I'll come back. But it's fine to take the other animals back to their regular locations. Could you have some staffers come check on Mika every hour or so?"

"Count me in," Josh said.

Janna wasn't surprised, but she did smile at him, and found him already smiling at her. She would definitely look forward to seeing him when she returned tomorrow. Or tonight, although she hoped Mika would do well enough not to require a visit.

"Will do," Scott said, "although you won't be the only one who'll peek in on Mika tonight, Josh. You'll need to come get the clinic key from me now and then, then bring it back to my office."

"Of course."

"Let's put Mika in an enclosure and get the other animals out so you can return them to their normal areas in the shelter," Janna said. She was pleased, but not surprised, when Josh lifted Mika off the table and held her. She was also not surprised when Nella reached over and gently patted Mika on her unhurt side.

Next, they headed toward the room where Elmer and Pekie were in their enclosures. Janna pointed out one of the other enclosures to Josh and opened its gate, rearranging the fluffy dog bed inside so Josh could gently place Mika onto it.

Nella and Scott each took one of the other dogs out of their enclosures and put leashes on them. Both Pekie and Elmer seemed happy and energetic, ready to go.

Janna soon had Squeegee on a leash, which she handed to Josh. Then she went into a separate room to get Furball.

"I can carry her," she told Scott and Nella. "We'll take all of them but Mika outside here now, and you can have Josh and other staff members bring them to their usual kennels, okay?"

"That's exactly what we'll do," Nella agreed.

While she still held Furball, Janna got Wizzy from his enclosure. She put the cat down for a moment while she attached Wizzy's leash, then joined the others who were waiting to leave.

"Let me take one more peek at Mika," she told them, handing Furball to Nella and Wizzy's leash to Josh.

Fortunately, the pup appeared to be asleep, breathing normally. She left a bowl of water and another with a little kibble in the enclosure, both raised on a stand a bit so she'd be able to reach them even with the cone.

"See you tomorrow, sweetie," Janna said, then left.

Scott and Nella walked out of the clinic first, each holding a dog's leash, as was Josh. Nella also held Furball and Janna, of course, had Wizzy's leash.

She made sure the clinic door was locked behind her. Josh and others would be given the key briefly to go check on Mika later.

Scott and Josh had begun talking together softly. Something in the uneasy look on Josh's face suggested he was speaking to the director about what they'd talked about earlier—the threats against him. Janna was glad Josh—Nolan—was here for his protection.

There wasn't much she could do to help him other than worry, but at least he should be okay here.

Right?

Well, time for her to leave. She'd look forward to confirming he remained okay when she returned tomorrow.

Josh was sorry to see Janna leave but he knew it was doubtful that he'd get to spend any more time with her that day, even if she had stayed to keep an eye on Mika, the injured dog.

He was a staff member here now, after all. He had work to accomplish other than Nolan's writing. He had to help take care of the animals under the shelter's care, like Mika. And like Squeegee, whose leash he now held.

At least, he'd been able to say a quick goodbye to Janna as she left with Wizzy.

"Let's put these two in the same enclosure," Scott said of Squeegee and Elmer. The chocolate Lab mix was of similar size to Elmer, a retriever mix, so they would both reside in the building for medium-size dogs. "Then we'll find you a staff member or two to work with this afternoon, walking some dogs and working with them more on learning commands."

"Fine," Josh said.

In a softer voice, even though no one was nearby to hear them, Scott added, "And be sure to keep me informed of other things you hear about…your life outside, if anything. I'll get in touch with some of my local contacts now and let them know what you told me, and they'll step up the patrols around here as a precaution."

Josh knew Scott was talking about the local police. Scott was one himself, undercover. "I appreciate it," he said, even though he didn't believe whoever was threatening him knew he was here. But it didn't hurt to be careful.

He noticed some staff members outside near the buildings, giving commands to the dogs with them to train. As he would soon be doing.

Managers Telma and Camp and staffer Chessie were in the building for medium-sized dogs when Josh and Scott walked in. Young Leonard was also there. Josh had met him but hadn't yet spoken with him.

"Hi, all of you," Chessie said. "How are Elmer and Squeegee doing?"

"Well enough to start resting here," Scott said. "Maybe tomorrow you and some of the others can start walking them again."

"Fine. Leonard and I came in to pick our afternoon companions, but we won't choose those two."

"How about Ashy and Spike?" Leonard asked, looking into one of the enclosures. Several dogs had come to the gate, apparently wanting attention.

"Sounds good to me," Chessie said.

"Pick out one more," Scott said. "Josh is going to join you."

In a short while, the three of them left with three dogs: Chessie was in charge of the gray poodle Ashy, Leonard was walking Moe, a black Lab mix, and Josh had the leash of former K-9 Spike, a German shepherd. Scott followed them out the door but, after wishing them a good afternoon, headed for his office.

They started down a walkway with tall fencing all around. No one could see in or out. Nice and safe, Josh thought.

"Hey," Chessie said suddenly.

"Hey what?" Josh asked and glanced at her. The young woman had short, light hair and green eyes. Today, she was in a gray Chance Animal Shelter shirt that went well with Ashy. As with everyone he'd met in the short time he'd been at the shelter, Josh wondered what had brought her here but of course wouldn't ask.

"Hey, how are you doing, new staffer?" Chessie asked.

Josh laughed. "As well as all of you," he said. "Maybe even better."

"You can't be better than me," Leonard said. He had longish brown hair and hazel eyes that seemed to try to pierce into Josh's head, as if he wanted to learn what had brought Josh there. But he, too, apparently knew better than to ask. "This place is my good friend."

"Guess it's also becoming mine." Josh was enjoying himself, walking with these two people and all three dogs. Spike, he understood, was a retired K-9 who'd needed someplace to live. He helped keep watch over the place, just like directors Scott and Nella and the managers did.

As they walked, Josh, Chessie and Leonard sometimes stopped and gave commands to the dogs, common ones like sit, stay, come and heel. Apparently, that was one of the things the staff members here were supposed to do, to help get the dogs ready to be adopted—although Josh gathered that Spike was here to stay. But he figured the well-trained dog probably wouldn't mind being rewarded like the others with the treats Chessie had brought.

They neared the building where Josh had been earlier, helping Janna.

Too bad she wasn't there walking with them. But as a vet tech, and not someone in need of protection, she could come and go as she pleased. Josh couldn't help being a bit jealous.

Well, someday things would get worked out. Those outside, like Scott's police contacts, would be in touch with each other and determine who was threatening him and catch them.

Or at least that was how it would go if Nolan was writing the story.

And he couldn't help being himself even as he walked dogs at a shelter. His mind pondered the backgrounds of the people walking with him, even if he couldn't ask. How would he use them in a story? Not that he'd set anything at a shelter like this, not when it was so important to keep this secret. But even so...

Chessie and Leonard had stopped walking again, so Josh did too. "Ashy, sit," Chessie said to her poodle companion, and the dog obeyed. Leonard did the same with Moe, so Josh figured it was his turn and did the same with Spike. No surprise. The shepherd did as told, looking straight into Josh's eyes. He fortunately got a treat from Chessie and gave it to his canine companion.

Close to dinnertime, Leonard suggested they take the dogs back to their kennels. Josh made sure Spike was settled back in his enclosure, then, even though it wasn't his responsibility, he couldn't help checking on Elmer and Squeegee. Fortunately, they both looked okay too.

In the cafeteria, Josh followed his new routine and got his meal from the food counter. There was no room at the table to sit with Scott and Nella that night, but maybe it was just as well. He remained with his afternoon companions, joining Leonard, Chessie and a bunch of other staff members at their long table.

It all felt nice and calm and safe. No reason for Josh to think about what had brought him here, the threats online he'd gotten since arriving or anything else.

Only…he did think about it. Worry about it. It was who he was. He wanted his real life back as soon as possible.

And he wanted to write about all that had happened to him, all the threats, and come up with answers as to who was behind them, real or not. He wanted to write a good story—and hopefully discover the culprit at the same time.

But none of that would happen right now.

At the moment, he couldn't help thinking about how

enjoyable it had been to share the few meals he'd had here with Janna. He'd at least get to see her again tomorrow when she returned to the clinic for work.

And tonight—well, it should be a nice, calm night to just hang out in his apartment here. Maybe he'd even get a little writing done, or at least make some notes about what would happen next. Or maybe he'd work on something altogether new, not related to his most recent book or what was going on in his life. A nice, nasty mystery straight out of his imagination.

"You okay?" Beside him, Chessie leaned over as she ate, looking at him in concern.

"Heck yes," he said. "Just enjoying this great hamburger and pondering all the fun I had this afternoon walking with Leonard and you and the dogs."

"That's great," she said. "I liked it too. And I also like this hamburger, although I think it could use a bit more cheese."

Josh laughed. Yes, this felt nice and relaxing. Was it the calm before the next storm? He certainly hoped not.

But later that evening, when he returned to his apartment, he took care to lock the door before he booted up his computer.

He first checked his social media. There was a bit of positive new input regarding his latest release. Readers were sharing information about it and posting reviews. Not everyone loved it, but that was okay. Everything helped get word out there, and nothing was too terrible. No nastiness in any of it this time.

He held his breath a little as he opened his email. Many of the threats he'd gotten had shown up there. But there was nothing new since he'd checked that morning. He started breathing again.

He noticed something from his publicist, Roger Meltry of Meltry Media. He was in no hurry to open that one. So far, the publicity had been working well. His book was definitely out there in the public eye. Of course, Josh was always happy to help his books become bestsellers. This one seemed on its way, but it was too early to be sure.

While he was checking his emails, a few new ones came in. Some were the usual spam and ads, but one was from his agent, Bruce Ashcourt.

Nothing new or different there. Josh really appreciated his agent, who was always eager to look at new ideas from him, then get out there and sell them to good publishers. Of course, with Nolan's reputation for writing books that became bestsellers, he figured Bruce had good reason to appreciate him too. But Josh also valued Bruce's ideas and hard work to make sure he sold Nolan's manuscripts to the right place.

Today, Bruce was just checking in, saying that he too had been seeing good reviews and indications that *Murder for Dinner* was continuing to sell well. He also asked how Nolan was doing.

Bruce knew about the threats, of course, since he'd received some directed at Nolan. Josh had let Bruce know he was leaving town for a while for his safety without letting him know where he was going. The fewer people who knew, the better, even among those he trusted.

Josh sent Bruce a response, indicating he was still

fine and hanging out someplace he believed to be safe without giving any details.

Finally, he returned to Roger's email. That one disturbed him—badly. His publicist indicated there'd been lots of correspondence with book retailers, asking where Nolan Hoffsler would be appearing to promote his new book and do signings. In the past, Nolan had done that a lot, traveling to major cities and visiting the largest stores with the most buying traffic.

But he could hardly do that now. If whoever was threatening him was serious about harming him, or worse, it would no longer be difficult for them to find him.

Roger had also received some threats directed at Nolan. Josh drafted a response, reminding the publicist why he wanted to stay out of the public eye.

But an idea started forming in his mind. What if he could provide signed books at a lot of locations? Or at least provide stickers for booksellers to place inside books. He could sign stickers in advance so purchasers could still have signed copies of his book—sort of.

He had quite a few with him. It was something he always carried, no matter where he went. Even into protective custody, as it turned out.

The idea started to gel more in his mind.

There were problems with it, though. He usually handed out the stickers in person. Sometimes he mailed a bunch to booksellers in areas he wasn't visiting or wouldn't get to for a while. Now, there was no way he could take them to a post office personally.

He'd have to ponder that further. Maybe he could get

Janna to help? Another reason to get together with her alone to talk. He intended to finish reading her manuscript that night anyway.

He'd have to give scheduling some time with her more of an effort tomorrow.

Chapter 8

It had been an interesting rest of the afternoon at the downtown Chance Animal Clinic. Someone had brought in a pregnant cat in labor, and Janna helped to deliver the kittens safely. All four babies appeared in good condition, which thrilled the owner, a Chance resident, but the mom seemed to be having a slightly difficult time breathing. Janna had alerted one of the vets, and the cat and kittens were remaining overnight under the observation of another vet tech.

Finally, Janna and Wizzy were relaxing in her condo near downtown Chance. She'd lived there for a couple of months and was really fond of the nice development it was part of. Half a dozen two-story buildings were arranged around a well-maintained garden. Her unit was on the ground floor.

It had been an hour or so since their arrival home. "You ready to go out again?" she asked Wizzy.

Her adorable Australian shepherd mix barked his positive response—fortunately, in this condo, not too loudly.

And so they went outside again for what would likely be the penultimate yard visit for the day. Janna came prepared for cleaning, and they soon went back into their unit.

"Dinnertime!" she told Wizzy, who did excited circles in the kitchen. Janna fed him first, then got ready for her own meal. As always, she had a few ready-made things available for dinner—a premade salad plus a frozen meal of salmon, rice and asparagus, all somewhat healthy. She'd always enjoyed cooking, but not just for herself.

Her mind meandered to whom she'd really like to invite over for dinner. But there was no way Josh would be able to visit her here.

She enjoyed hanging out at the shelter for meals. The food there was okay, and she liked the staff members and Scott and Nella. And Kyle, of course, but her boss seldom ate at the shelter cafeteria, since he preferred to spend time with his K-9 cop girlfriend, Maisie. Janna occasionally joined other technicians for lunch or dinner downtown and always had fun discussing patients and more with them. But though she was definitely friends with them, they didn't tend to hang out a lot since most of her coworkers were married.

Not that Janna was in any hurry to find a husband. But…

Her thoughts suddenly turned to the man she'd recently become quite attracted to, and not just because he was a best-selling author with wonderful books. Get to know him better? Sure. Get his writing advice? Absolutely. But no way would they ever develop a relationship, let alone one that could lead to marriage.

Although the thought certainly was intriguing. Especially considering who he was…

She laughed aloud at herself, and Wizzy, who'd been lying on the floor near the kitchen table as she prepared her dinner, came over and wagged his tail.

"Just letting my imagination go wild, boy," she told him, and he wagged some more.

Someday soon, she'd plan ahead to stay overnight at the vet apartment at the shelter and bring some good things along to cook. Someday when she could invite Josh to join her.

She wished she could talk to him this evening, even just a phone call to say goodnight. But staff members didn't have phones. They weren't supposed to make phone calls. On the other hand, Josh did have computer access, unlike other staff members, but she didn't have his email address.

Oh, well. She was assigned to the downtown clinic first the next day, but later on she'd visit the shelter.

For tonight, she had to conduct her life as it was before she met the handsome novelist. She read a couple of chapters in her manuscript, then watched some news and a show about animal care and welfare. When she finally went to bed, she lay awake for a while, once more thinking about Josh. What would he be thinking about as he prepared to go to bed?

No. No thinking about joining him there ever, no matter how sexy he was.

But would he be pondering the plot of a new book? Would he be thinking about the terrible threats that had brought him to the shelter? Both? After all, he'd apparently used a real murder as a background for his latest novel, and that had gotten him into trouble. But it made sense for a wonderful novelist like him to take things in his own life and use them as a background for fiction.

Hopefully, since he was a staffer now, he would remain safe, no matter what those threats were about and who sent them.

Another thing for her to talk to him about—whenever she had the opportunity to talk to him about writing. She hoped it would be tomorrow.

Still, she couldn't help glancing at the other side of her queen-size bed. What it would be like to have Josh there? She'd had men in her life before. She knew what it was like to go to bed with them—and more.

And she couldn't help thinking that *more* would be the watchword if she ever happened to get the opportunity to be with Josh that way. Or was that a dream that would only come true in her imagination—like getting her own book published?

Drat. No use getting pessimistic.

Still, she whispered out loud, "Good night, Josh."

Of course Wizzy heard her. She'd just taken him out for his last venture of the night, and he snuggled against her.

She patted his head. "Sleep well, pup."

And she saw Josh's handsome face in her mind again before she drifted off to sleep.

In the morning, she went through her usual routine of showering, getting dressed, grabbing a quick breakfast and heading to the downtown clinic with Wizzy. She checked first on the mama cat and her kittens. The vet tech who'd stayed overnight, Betty, assured her they were doing fine.

Janna was assigned to work as Kyle's assistant that day, as she often was. The morning went fast, as usual. Soon it was time to grab lunch and head to the shelter clinic. Kyle would be there an hour or so later, but she'd check on Mika, the single animal currently in the clinic, then walk around to make sure all the other shelter animals were doing okay.

Maybe, when she brought Wizzy out to play with some of the staffers, she could see how they were doing and ask if they believed all the animals in their care were healthy. Normal stuff.

And if she happened to run into Josh? Well, she'd be glad to see him, as she was the other staff members, but that was all.

She had to make sure that was all.

Janna parked in her usual spot just outside the shelter's tall fencing and called the office. Nella soon came to open the gate and let her and Wizzy in.

The assistant director locked the gate behind them, then knelt as she often did to hug Janna's dog. "Welcome, Wizzy," she said, then stood. "And welcome, Janna."

"How is Mika doing today?" Janna asked. She figured the beagle mix must be doing alright or someone at the shelter would have called Kyle—and he'd probably have sent Janna here right away to check on her.

"She seems fine. I've looked in on her a few times, plus I fed her breakfast. Some staffers looked in on her too and one even took her for a short walk when I okayed it. I figured it'd be all right since she was favoring her sore side, but with the cone still on, she wasn't licking it, and I thought the attention would be good."

"Sounds good to me," Janna agreed. She hurried to the clinic to take a look at Mika.

The poor pup clearly wasn't happy with the cone, since she shook her head as soon as Janna came close.

"Let's take a look," Janna said, and let Mika out. She removed the cone and placed the pup on an examination table. Holding Mika steady, she gently removed the bandage from her injury. It had definitely improved. "But Dr. Kornel has to make the decision whether you can be let loose without the cone. For now, you need to get bandaged up again and stay here, cone on."

Then it was time to do rounds for the rest of the shelter animals, at least till Kyle arrived in an hour or so. And maybe she could see which staffers happened to be around.

"Okay, Wiz, let's go," she said, picking up her dog from his own enclosure and locking the clinic door behind them.

Janna wasn't surprised to see an array of shelter dogs out and about on leashes, being led by, or leading, quite a few staffers.

She didn't really know how many people were under protection here, appearing to the outside world as homeless people hired to care for the animals inside. All of them helped to teach newcomers and work with each other, and they all seemed to do a fantastic job of caring for the animals.

Small animals like guinea pigs and rabbits were taken out of their enclosures several times a day and petted and given food and attention. The cats received even more attention, so they'd be socialized and ready to enjoy their new homes once they were adopted.

But it was the dogs who got the most attention, which Janna understood. They tended to be smart and needed activity, but they also appeared to like humans as much as humans liked them. They seemed to enjoy training, learning human commands and how to obey them. Just like Wizzy did.

On the shelter's center path, Bibi was walking Mocha, a little terrier mix she often helped train. Nearby, Denise was walking Oodles, a white dog who appeared part poodle.

"Hi, Janna," Bibi called, waving and smiling.

"Yes, hi." Denise's smile was even larger than Bibi's, wide against her dark skin.

Janna felt warmed by their greeting, as contact with staff members generally did. "Everyone seem to be doing okay?" she asked, referring to the animals the women were walking.

"Definitely," Bibi said.

"We'd let Scott or Nella know if we saw that any of them needed your help," Denise added.

"I figured," Janna said with a smile. She joined them on their walk, which Wizzy always seemed to really enjoy. She tried to give him as much exercise and attention as she could when she wasn't busy at the clinic. Plus, he recognized some of the staffers' names, and she often told him to go see Bibi and Denise and others when they were out with shelter dogs.

After a while, though, Janna figured it was time to

head back to the clinic so she'd be there when Kyle arrived. "See you later," she told Bibi and Denise and led Wizzy back the way they'd come.

Janna couldn't help feeling glad when she saw Josh exiting the office building and heading her direction. She'd at least get a chance to say hi.

He was walking Spike, the German shepherd, and he lifted a hand in greeting. "Hi, Janna," he said. "And how are you today, Wizzy?"

"Say hi to Josh," Janna told her pup as they drew closer.

Josh bent to give Wizzy a pat on the head, then did the same for Spike. Both pups seemed happy for the attention, wagging their tails.

Josh's long-sleeved Chance Animal Shelter shirt today was a deep blue, and it hugged his muscular chest—as all the T-shirts here appeared to. Janna knew she shouldn't pay attention, so she looked up into his brown eyes instead.

"We're both doing fine," Janna told him. "How about you?"

"Fine also. And..." He paused. "Well, I'd really like for you to come to my apartment later. After dinner, maybe, if that works for you. I've been pondering a time when we can talk about your—you know."

A couple of staffers were walking near them, fortunately not close enough to hear Josh's lowered voice. Even so, Janna appreciated his discretion in not mentioning her manuscript. Of course, that also helped him keep his own identity private, even though she might have asked anyone to review her work.

"That should be fine," she said, also quietly. She attempted not to sound too excited, but she was thrilled she was finally going to get Nolan Hoffsler's comments about her writing. "I still have work to do at the clinic this afternoon, but I can hang around after dinner."

"Very good. In fact, I'll go to the cafeteria first and bring some food up to my place so we can eat dinner there. I won't say I'm sharing with someone else, just that I want enough to eat later."

Janna laughed. "Guess it's better not to mention you'll have company, or Sara the cook may wonder who and why."

"Exactly. So how about if I head to the clinic around five? Then I can bring you and Wizzy to my unit."

"Sounds good," Janna said. "I'll close the clinic then unless there's an emergency."

"Oh, and there's something I want to talk to you about in addition to your story," he said. "Something from my perspective. See you soon."

Before she could respond, Josh turned and gave Spike the command to come. Janna was left to wonder what else they'd be discussing that night.

The idea of being alone with Josh in his apartment stimulated her imagination.

She shook it off, laughing at herself. "Let's go to the clinic, Wizzy," she said, and started walking in the opposite direction from Josh and Spike.

For now, at least.

She'd be there. Josh couldn't be happier.

Oh, that was primarily because he was going to do his

best to recruit her into helping him get his book-signing materials mailed out.

He'd been hoping to find a good time to get together with Janna to discuss her manuscript, of course, and he wanted to do his best to help her. But now he also needed her assistance. It would involve some of her time, but it shouldn't be dangerous for her.

And it would definitely be helpful for him.

For the next few hours, though, he had to comply with his obligations here at the shelter, and that involved working with Spike a while longer. Josh was glad he'd been given the former K-9 as his shelter companion, flattered in a way. All staffers were obliged to train the dogs under their care, but Spike was doing a good job of training Josh.

He wanted to give the dog one more walk up the center pathway and back before returning him to his kennel for the evening. And working with Spike was a good way to avoid anticipating his time alone with Janna later.

Although he couldn't help thinking about it…

Even though he found the vet tech attractive, that was irrelevant. They each had a goal for meeting that evening.

He recalled her manuscript well, plus he'd made notes on things to improve. Not that he was an expert on others' writing, but he believed she had a good shot at ultimately getting it published.

And if he could get her help in return, it might save his career, or at least hopefully keep it from fading for lack of publicity.

At the end of the walkway, Josh turned and said,

"Spike, heel." The K-9 responded perfectly, and soon, they were back in the building for medium-size dogs.

Other staffers were directing the pups in their possession to return to their appropriate enclosures, rewarding them with treats. A few staff members would return after they'd had their own dinners to feed the dogs their evening meals and give them one last outing of the evening.

"In, Spike," Josh commanded. The shepherd understood and walked into the enclosure, turning to look back at Josh, who handed him one of the treats in his pocket. "Good boy," he said. "I hope we get to walk again soon."

"Hey, I like Spike too," said Augie, who'd come up beside him without a dog. The senior must have already gotten his companion for that afternoon into his enclosure.

"Well, I know he gets the companionship of a lot of staffers here besides me," Josh said. "Hopefully you're among them."

"Sometimes," Augie replied, then added, "Looks like the others here are heading to the cafeteria. Want to join me for dinner?"

"I'll walk that way with you," Josh said, "but I have some things I need to take care of in my apartment tonight, so I'll just be picking up my dinner. I'd like to join you for another meal, though, one of these days."

"Sounds good." And Augie walked off to catch up with some of the other staff members, probably wanting to work out a dinner companion for the night. He was fairly spry for his age. Josh was glad he didn't seem upset at Josh's rejection.

In the cafeteria, Josh went right away to the food counter. Chef Sara was there, watching the crowd plate their own meals from the things she'd prepared.

"Evening," Josh greeted her. "Do you happen to have any containers I can use to take food back to my apartment? In fact, I'd like to take enough for a couple of evenings. I just need some alone time." He didn't explain why or that he wouldn't exactly be alone.

"Sure," she said. "A lot of staff members sometimes decide they want to eat alone. I even give them unprepared items of food that they can cook themselves if they wish. But taking something already prepared is fine too. Wait here."

She headed toward the kitchen and returned shortly with a nice-size empty container with a lid.

"Thanks a lot," Josh told her, then got into the line.

Bibi and Chessie stood near him, but if they noticed he was holding a container rather than a plate, neither said anything. Instead, they continued their own conversation about the dogs they worked with that day. Each seemed to be bragging about their training skills, which amused Josh.

He filled his container with the entrée that night, a thick stew of vegetables and beef. He had some bread in his apartment as well as bottled water, and figured that should be sufficient.

Then it was time to head to the clinic. If anyone asked, he could always say he was concerned about Mika. And that he cared a lot about any animals needing veterinary care, so he just wanted to check on them there before heading up to his apartment for the night.

But fortunately, no one appeared to notice or care when he left. At the door to the clinic, he knocked with his free hand that wasn't holding the food container.

In less than a minute, Janna opened the door.

"Hi," he said. "How's Mika?" Hey, he did actually give a damn about the dog.

"She's doing well. She might even be able to go back to the shelter tomorrow, after we clean and bandage her again."

We. Well, sure, she was referring to Dr. Kornel.

"That's great. Could I take a peek at her?"

"Of course."

Janna directed him inside the dog's enclosure. Mika was probably still somewhat sedated since she remained lying down. He didn't say anything to disturb her but quietly walked back out.

"So," he said to Janna, "ready for dinner?" He held up the container.

"Sounds good," she said. "And some writing tips too, I hope. Let's go get Wizzy and head to your apartment?"

"Definitely."

Fortunately, they didn't run into any staff members on the way. Otherwise, Josh might have had to figure out what to tell them. He didn't have any animals with him or in his apartment. And having dinner alone together in his apartment with the shelter's vet tech? There was certainly something suggestive about that, even though it was really just a meeting between two people who wanted something from each other. And not in a sexy way either. Which was kind of a shame.

After letting Wizzy sniff around outside for a couple

of minutes, they hurried up the stairs to his fourth-floor unit. He quickly unlocked the door and ushered his visitors in first.

"Let me get our dinner warmed up, then we can sit at the table and talk about your manuscript as we eat. And when we're done, we can talk about what I want to discuss with you—how you can possibly help me save my career."

He was joking. Sort of. But he loved the startled look on her face.

"How could I possibly—" she began.

"Like I said, we'll talk about it later. Hey, are you hungry? I am. And we should be able to give a little of the meat in this stew to Wizzy, if that's all right with you."

"Fine."

And Josh hoped they would each have as productive an evening as they anticipated.

Chapter 9

"Sure, giving Wizzy a little bit of stew should be fine," Janna said. "I'll need to look it over first to be sure, though, and limit the amount."

Wow, she thought as they followed him into the kitchen. It was finally happening. She was alone with Nolan Hoffsler tonight in his apartment. He was going to give her his opinion of her manuscript and suggest how to improve it.

Nolan Hoffsler, the best-selling author!

And an exceptionally good-looking and sexy guy...

Well, that part was irrelevant, even though it was intriguing. That wasn't why they were hanging out tonight. Although there was something he wanted to talk to her about too. She wondered what it was.

Nolan—yes, for tonight, he was Nolan in her mind and not Josh—placed the container of food on the counter. "Okay," he said, and removed a couple of plates from a cabinet. Plain ones but sturdy, as was the norm for the apartments at the shelter.

Nolan dished out servings of stew from the container, nearly emptying it, but Janna noticed he set aside several large clumps of meat for Wizzy.

"Is this okay?" He turned and gestured to the spread on the counter. "I'll get a bowl for Wizzy, too."

Janna examined the meat he'd left out for Wizzy, then the stew.

Nolan remained close enough to look on over her shoulder.

Oh, yes, she was well aware of his nearness. Even though he'd been suggestive of nothing beyond feeding her dog and having their own supper.

"Looks good," she said, "although I'll give Wizzy a cooked carrot and some beans too. They're fine for him to eat, and he'll enjoy them."

Nolan pulled out two wide blue plastic bowls, and Janna spooned some stew into one for her dog. Wizzy started eating as soon as she placed the bowl on the floor. She filled the other bowl with water and set that down as well.

Meanwhile, Nolan placed flatware and napkins on the table, then poured glasses of water for them. He gestured for her to begin eating.

"I know you want my opinion of your manuscript," Nolan began, looking her straight in the eyes and holding a spoonful of stew just above his plate.

"Definitely." Janna stopped in the middle of taking a bite from her plate. Would she even want to eat after this?

"Now, you know I'm just another writer…" When Janna opened her mouth to protest the word *just*, he continued, "Yes, I'm successful at it, and proud of it. And I really think you're off to a wonderful start on your story. I believe you'll be able to get it into a good publishing house soon, if that's what you'd like." He didn't wait for her to respond about what she really wanted, although that was most likely obvious. "But here are some of my thoughts about how to improve it to make it even easier to get it published."

The concept had appeal, she thought. A murder mystery with a female cop who'd been pulled into a very difficult case—one in which she wound up getting involved romantically with one of the suspects.

"The plot works well for me," he said, "but there are times your protagonist just dives into her investigation in a way that suggests all she wants to do is to clear her potential love interest of any suspicion. Which is understandable, but you obviously want her to be a good cop, so she needs to be more careful about how she approaches it. She also should be willing to step back if it becomes clearer that the guy she likes is guilty."

"I thought I had done that, but maybe not as well as I should have. Did you happen to mark pages where you had issues?"

"Yes, I did, and I finished reading it last night," he said. "I also made notes on some ways I thought things could progress better. And how their relationship began and continued... Well, I really liked that, at least of what I've read so far."

Nolan's look seemed almost suggestive. Had he been aroused by her writing? The heat from his gaze was turning her on.

She hurriedly went back to eating.

Nolan made some other suggestions, almost as if he had the manuscript in front of him. He'd clearly read it carefully. Janna understood and appreciated his comments, though she didn't necessarily agree with a few of them.

But she clearly still had a lot of work to do—not that she hadn't figured that before. She knew now even more of what she needed to change and add and clarify.

When they'd finished eating, Janna got up, disturbing Wizzy, who settled back down quickly. She removed a small notepad and pen from her purse and began jotting down notes.

"Oh, I've added comments to the manuscript," Nolan reminded her, "so you might not need to do that. I'll also go over the notes I made outside the manuscript with you later."

"But I've come up with some additional ideas of my own," she told him. "I can't thank you enough not only for reading it, but for giving me such detailed suggestions."

She ached to give him another kiss, she was so grateful. Good thing he still sat at the table. Approaching him that way would be even more awkward than if he happened to be standing beside her.

She had to ask, "When I'm done revising it, is there any possibility you'd be willing to take a look at it again?"

"Definitely. And at that point I could even make suggestions where you could submit it to possible agents or editors—maybe even mine, assuming I think it could be a fit for them. Considering how much I like it now, that's a good bet."

Janna was thrilled. He liked it well enough to suggest that his own contacts in the publishing industry might like it? Wow! But she knew better than to get her hopes up—at least not too high.

Still, she wanted to repay him in her own way. "Thank you so much. Now, what was it you wanted to talk to me about?" He'd joked about it being something that could save his career. Unlikely, but she'd do whatever she could to help him.

He explained his situation. He was unable to appear for book signings, but he could at least send signed stickers for booksellers to place inside his books. Would she be willing, he asked, to get him some more stickers, as well as envelopes and labels, then take them to a post office for him?

"Not the Chance post office, though," she said. "Just in case whoever's been threatening you learns about those stickers and tries to figure out where they were sent from."

"Exactly," he said with a huge smile. "We're on the same wavelength."

That wasn't the only thing they were on together. They were both standing by then, bringing dishes to the sink, and Janna suddenly felt herself drawn into Nolan's arms.

Or was she the one who moved first?

In any case, they went from looking deeply into each other's eyes to sharing a kiss—a kiss that stretched out long and hot. His way of thanking her in advance for helping save his career made her want to do a lot more with him.

Bad idea but intriguing.

After a nice long series of those amazing kisses, they both pulled gently away.

"I already have some ideas about how to get the things you'll need for me to mail the stickers and also how to send them," she said, knowing her voice sounded ragged. But despite the kiss, her mind had in fact been working. "Let's talk about it a little, okay?"

"Absolutely okay," he said, his voice throaty as well. He gave her another kiss—not nearly as heated this time, but sweet and gentle. "Let's talk."

Wow, Nolan thought. He'd sort of figured Janna would be willing to at least listen to his thoughts about how she could help him get things mailed. He hadn't expected her to jump in with her own suggestions.

And those kisses they'd shared? He couldn't stop thinking of them, even as they finished placing the dishes into the unit's small dishwasher. It was even harder to focus his thoughts when they sat on the gray sofa together in the living room. An oval coffee table stood between them and the TV mounted on the wall. Wizzy stretched out beside the sofa.

"So," Janna said, looking serious. "I'll go to a nearby office supply store soon to pick up a bunch of mailing envelopes, as well as some stickers for you to sign and some blank labels."

"Sounds good, but I don't want it obvious where the envelopes are coming from." Plus, he hoped to get it done quickly. It'd be too complicated and time-consuming to ask his agent or publicist for this kind of help.

"That's the fun of the plan I've come up with. When we get all of the envelopes labeled for the retailers you want to receive them, I'll head for a post office in another town that's not too far away. I'll put the envelopes inside a couple large mailers. And guess whose names and addresses I'll put on those." She laughed. "No way you'll be able to guess."

He was puzzled, but he smiled back at her. "Okay, tell me."

"Well, I've got a couple of sisters who live fairly far away, in Chicago and Miami. We're pretty close, and they won't ask questions if I tell them what I'm doing is secret. I'll send the two large mailers to April and Chloe, and they'll drop the smaller ones inside them into their local mail. And we won't put your name on the outside of those smaller envelopes, just inside on a printed note for the booksellers to read."

"You got this figured out in no time," he said, his head tilted slightly as he looked at her. "I'm impressed." And he really was. There was little chance that anyone looking for him would be able to figure out where the stickers with his signatures came from—even if whoever it was heard about his books being "signed" in a variety of places all over the country.

But he couldn't help adding, "As much as I appreciate your help, though, I worry about whether your complicity in this will be obvious. Could someone figure out that you know where I am?"

And potentially attack her instead of him—but he didn't mention that. He didn't want to worry her. But he'd quash this whole idea if it seemed to get too dangerous for Janna.

"Oh, I'll definitely be careful around here and in communicating with my sisters," she said easily. "Show me the stickers you have before I leave, and I'll try to find similar ones. I should be able to pick up the stuff at different locations tomorrow, not all in Chance, although it might take us a day or two to get everything addressed. I'll call my sisters early tomorrow to warn them I have a chore for them to do and how it has to be confidential. They won't see the notes and signed stickers inside the smaller envelopes I'll ask them to mail. They won't mind helping."

"They sound like nice sisters," Nolan said.

"They are. And—well, you probably know the feeling even more than I do, but as a writer, I tend to think about what's going on in my life that I can include in a story. This idea of obscuring the location you're mailing from sounds like something to include in a novel. But I know better than to do anything that could make it look like I know someone who's in hiding."

Nolan couldn't help agreeing. "What we're doing here has to remain secret, at least till it's figured out who's been threatening me and that person has been apprehended."

"I get it," Janna said. "But this has to be over with eventually. Meantime I'll just let my mind wander over possibly plotting a fictional version."

He was amused, though, and even a bit impressed. "It sounds as if you already have at least some of the inner thoughts of a longtime writer. Potentially a successful one."

"Darn, I hope so. I want to keep on being a vet tech too since I love helping animals, but taking time in my own mind to create stories that other people may like to read—I love it!"

He loved her attitude. Under other, better circumstances, he might even allow himself to develop feelings for her. He was already attracted to her. And here they were, alone in his apartment, at least for a while longer...

No. He was smart. He was sane. And so he stifled his lust, or at least tried to, and continued to discuss what he hoped to achieve: lots of people having his signature in the new books they bought, even without meeting him.

"Sorry I didn't bring dessert," he eventually said to change the subject. "But it wouldn't be a good idea for us to go to the cafeteria together to get some. Besides, I figure you need to go home to get some rest—and plan your schedule for tomorrow." Like, how to work around when stores would be open for her to get supplies.

"My intention is to get up early to go to the downtown clinic, then leave earlier than usual before heading here. In between, I should be able to get all the stuff we'll need. Now..." She stood up from the sofa, and Wizzy rose from the floor beside her. "Show me the stickers you have, then I'll leave."

Only, when he stood up and faced her, there was something suggestive in her expression. Something that reminded him of their earlier kisses.

Without allowing himself to consider how reckless it might be, he pulled her into his arms again. Closer this time.

He reveled in the feel of her warm, curvaceous body against him as he lowered his head and kissed her again.

Longer than the last time. Hotter, as his hands began to roam against her, touching her back and sliding lower.

Her moan was soft against his mouth.

His mind darted to the possibilities. The couch was too small for real enjoyment, but his bedroom wasn't far away in this tiny apartment.

But before he could lead her there, or even make the suggestion, she pulled away. She looked at him with her lovely green eyes. "Wow," she said. "I'll have a lot to think about tonight, but Wizzy and I need to leave now. Tomorrow will be a busy day."

"Right," Nolan said, stepping back a little more. "I can't tell you how much I appreciate all you'll be doing for me."

"Your help with my writing is definitely thanks enough," she said, her voice stronger now. "Oh, and by the way, I'll obviously need to bring all the supplies here to your apartment so we can work on getting things ready. Maybe dinner here again tomorrow? And you may want to alert Scott about what's going on, so it won't seem too odd for me to be around outside the usual clinic times when no animals need ongoing help—which I hope none will tomorrow."

"Good idea," Nolan said, although he'd already planned to tell Scott about how Janna would be helping him. And the idea of being alone with her here in his unit again tomorrow night…?

He had to remain sane. They'd be busy with the mailing supplies Janna would bring, plus he still had to give her all the addresses to print on the labels. No time for anything more.

No time for them to grow any closer.

He would just have to keep his sanity.

Which was a shame, he thought as he showed Janna the stickers he already had, then gave her some money to pay for the new supplies.

He accompanied Janna and Wizzy to his door and went outside first to ensure no one was in the hallway to see them. Then he watched as they started down the stairs.

Without him.

Chapter 10

It was too late to head to a post office by the time Janna left the shelter that night, but some discount stores probably remained open. She and Wizzy made a quick stop in the clinic to check on Mika one last time.

Fortunately the little beagle mix seemed to be doing well. She still had her cone on, but Janna figured it could be removed for a while tomorrow when she was there to make sure the pup didn't try chewing at her bandaged wound.

Next, Janna called Nella to ask her to let her out. She didn't volunteer why she had stayed so long. The directors and staff were used to Kyle and the vet techs leaving late if there were any animals under observation.

Nella was still dressed in a shelter shirt and nice slacks when she met up with Janna and Wizzy at the clinic and walked them to the door. The expression on her face indicated she cared that Janna had stayed so late but obviously figured it was to take care of Mika.

Janna didn't tell her otherwise. She certainly didn't mention Josh and the things they'd discussed in his apartment—or anything else they'd done there, although the thought got Janna's heart rate up a bit. If there'd been any need for her to take more care of the shelter's animals, she would have been glad for any excuse to hang around and maybe see Josh again tonight…

Not going to happen. But she could look forward to the next day.

Meanwhile, she could start the preparations she had discussed with Josh.

"Thanks," she said to Nella as the assistant director let her and Wizzy out. "See you tomorrow."

After fastening Wizzy carefully in the back seat, Janna called to him, "Now, let's go shopping." In the rearview mirror, she saw him wag his tail.

There were a couple of stores Janna considered stopping at in Chance, especially since it was getting late, but instead she drove about half an hour to a town farther north. At a large office supply store, she picked up some bubble mailers and labels and some stickers that weren't as ornate as Nolan's but were okay. She'd left Wizzy locked in the car with the windows down a bit. It certainly wasn't too hot at that hour, and she'd be less obvious without him at her side.

She paid with cash Nolan had given her, and she and Wizzy were soon headed back to her condo.

Fortunately, it wasn't too late to call her sisters. No details yet, but she wanted to let each of them know she needed their help.

Sitting at her kitchen table, she called April first. Her older sister lived in Chicago and worked for an advertising agency—clearly successfully, since she lived well. Plus, she was engaged, though Janna didn't know of any wedding plans yet.

"Hi, Janna. What's going on?" April asked immediately, which wasn't surprising. Of all of them, she'd always been the most curious.

But Janna just said, "I'm calling to ask you to do something. It involves a secret. A practical joke." One that involved a very special man...but she definitely couldn't mention that. "I'll let you know more when I can. It just involves receiving a large package and taking the smaller envelopes inside to your local post office to mail. Will you help?"

Of course her loving big sister said yes.

Her younger sister, Chloe, lived in Miami. The divorced manager of a high-end clothing store was getting ready for bed, she said, since she needed to get up early. She seemed too distracted to ask many questions, but fortunately she agreed too.

After speaking with both of them, Janna was equal parts relieved and amused. She wished she could call Josh, let him know that things from her side seemed to be going well. But maybe it was better that she couldn't.

After a brief walk with Wizzy, then watching some TV, Janna lay in bed, still thinking about Josh. His comments about her manuscript had been wonderful, helpful and mostly complimentary. And he'd liked her suggestions about how to prepare and mail his stickers.

She would see him again tomorrow.

She lay there, thinking about him, and those kisses... They were likely to be alone again in his apartment the following evening.

Enough of that, she told herself.

But her mind kept going back to his kisses, his body against hers, even as she tried to fall asleep.

Eventually she was successful.

The next morning, she made herself wake up early. She walked and fed Wizzy, then grabbed cereal and milk for breakfast. Putting several large tote bags in the back of her SUV, she left for the downtown clinic.

It was busier than she'd hoped. Kyle immediately got her working with an aging shepherd mix who had apparently eaten some of his owner's chocolate. The poor dog had to have his stomach emptied, was fed charcoal to deal with the chocolate. Fortunately, he seemed to be okay, but Janna and another vet tech kept watch over him until it was time for Janna to head to the shelter.

Not that she and Wizzy went there right away. Instead, Janna again drove to another town, a different one from yesterday, and headed to the post office. No one seemed to pay any attention to her as she picked up an assortment of postal service mailers and stamps. And why should they? Picking up such things was normal at post offices, after all.

One of her totes already contained the envelopes, labels and stickers she'd bought yesterday. The mailers and stamps from the post office went into one of the others. Janna placed them on the floor behind the front seat of her black SUV where they couldn't easily be seen. Not that anyone would probably be nosy enough to look— but who knew?

Now it was off to Chance Animal Shelter's veterinary clinic. She was scheduled there for the whole afternoon and planned to stay for dinner. And somehow find a way to get this stuff to Josh's apartment.

She hoped by now he'd organized the names and addresses he wanted to put on the printed labels, but together they could make plans for what she should do next.

Which should take some time. Time with Josh. Oh, nothing would happen except for talking and planning—and maybe sneaking in a kiss or two again.

She could always hope.

Josh had been working with Spike at the shelter all day. Now it was the middle of the afternoon on a warm September day, a couple of hours after lunch.

Of course, he had been watching as much as he was able to for Janna's arrival. And not just because he was eager to get his eyes on the beautiful, sexy, smart vet tech again.

That too, of course, but he really wanted to know if she'd started collecting the pieces he'd need to get his signed stickers sent to booksellers.

No, what he really wanted was for things to get back to normal in his life so he could actually go do appearances and signings and not worry about any of this.

But he had to deal with things as they were—including staying safe, even hiding out here away from the jerk who had been threatening him.

If only it wasn't real. But from those attacks a while back—the fire and gunshots—plus all the communication that had been sent to him and others about him and hinted about on social media—okay. As much as he continued to overthink this, he couldn't take the chance.

"Spike, heel," he said as they continued down the shelter pathway with several other staffers and dogs. Chessie was again in charge of the gray poodle Ashy— unless Ashy was in charge of her. Leonard was with her walking Moe, the black Lab mix. Others were around too, including Augie. All this was the norm for a day at the shelter. It was a routine Josh enjoyed, but it wasn't who he was, even after being here a couple days.

What probably wasn't the norm was when Josh reached the end of the walkway near the main buildings and went inside each time, mostly indicating to anyone who seemed to wonder what he was up to that he was going to his apartment for a few minutes, or practicing a sudden change of plans from going in to out and back again. But he always headed to the vet clinic. He'd already seen Dr. Kornel there and said hello, asking how Mika was doing.

He did not mention to Dr. Kornel that he was more concerned about when Janna would arrive, hopefully bringing the supplies she'd promised.

Josh had already spoken with Scott about how he intended to mail signature stickers to hopefully keep his career going even when he couldn't conduct the appearances his publicist demanded. Scott had appeared concerned but said he would work out things so whatever Janna brought could be transferred to Josh's apartment without being observed by many, if any, curious staffers.

When Spike and Josh reached the apartment building once again, Josh told his walking companions, "I need to check on something at my apartment again."

The first time he'd left their walk that afternoon, he'd

said he wanted to go check on Mika in the clinic. Chessie had grinned at him. "I suspect it's not the poor pup you want to check on but a certain vet tech who'll be there sometime today, right?"

"Of course," he'd responded in a tone that suggested sarcasm. Even if it was true, it wasn't for the reason Chessie probably figured—that he was attracted to Janna.

Okay, he was, but he wasn't going to admit it. And that wasn't why he wanted—needed—to see her.

But after Chessie's comment, his excuse for going inside became wanting to grab something he'd forgotten from his apartment. Once he was inside and out of sight, he instead headed to the vet clinic, with Spike alongside him.

The first time, neither Dr. Kornel nor Janna were there yet. When no one replied to his knock, he'd left right away. He'd gone briefly to his apartment, as he'd indicated, then went back downstairs and started walking again with the staffers.

He repeated this a few times, and on the third, Dr. Kornel answered the door at Josh's knock. He assured Josh that Mika was okay and let him in to see her while Spike waited in the clinic lobby.

While Josh visited the little beagle mix, who seemed alert and curious, Dr. Kornel indicated that he expected Janna to arrive around three that afternoon. The vet seemed a little perturbed that she'd told him she needed a little time between the downtown clinic and the shelter without explaining why.

Josh knew the reason, of course, but he pretended to

be puzzled as well, though her hours weren't any of his concern. At least not as far as Dr. Kornel knew.

When it was finally approaching three o'clock, Josh and Spike once again reached the end of the shelter walkway.

"Hey, is your apartment expecting you again?" Chessie, again walking Ashy, was being sassy, but she was also clearly curious.

Josh definitely wasn't going to tell her the truth. "Guess so," was his reply, and he hurried into the building with the cafeteria downstairs and the apartments above.

Once again, he exited another door and headed to the vet clinic. With Spike still at his side, he once more checked to make sure no one was around watching him, then knocked on the clinic's door. Would Janna be there?

Again, he heard a male voice inside call out, "Just a second." Dr. Kornel opened the door, then stepped back so they could enter. He looked down at Spike. "He still looks fine, so I assume you're here to see Mika again— or Janna. Mika's still doing okay, and I just got a call from Janna that she'll be here in about ten minutes."

"Great," Josh said. "About both of them." He'd hoped Janna would finally be the one to let him into the clinic, but he wasn't surprised he'd been greeted by Dr. Kornel again. His mind quickly darted around until he added, "Janna and I have been discussing some things of interest to both of us. Like how to take care of the animals here."

He didn't want to mention her writing because she had told him not to. And he definitely didn't want to mention the wonderful help she was giving him.

"So I understand," was the vet's response, and he lifted his eyebrows as if he knew what Josh was talking about. Did he already know about Janna's writing? Was he aware that she knew who Josh actually was?

It didn't matter. Like everyone else around here, Dr. Kornel would be discreet even if he knew who Josh was. And if he knew about Janna's extracurricular interest, he would hopefully not give her a hard time about it. After all, Josh figured Janna wouldn't let her love of writing interfere with her vet tech career. She clearly cared a lot for animals.

Another good reason for Josh to care for her...

Okay, he had been here long enough. "Hey, Spike," he said to his companion, who was sitting beside him on the floor. "Time for us to leave."

But since Josh now had an idea of when to expect Janna, he hung around with Spike just inside the building, down the hall from the clinic.

Sure enough, Janna soon entered with Wizzy. She stopped and smiled when she saw them, and Josh smiled back.

"Hey," she said. "Good timing." She clearly didn't know he'd been coming here on and off to watch for her. "Let me go check in and get some work done. But let's get together here at dinner time. We can try to eat at Scott and Nella's table. Afterward, they should be able to help me get the things I brought up to your apartment without letting others know what's going on."

"Then you did bring the mailing supplies?" Josh couldn't help asking.

"Of course. I told you I would. But you need to sign

the stickers and tell me what to mail where, and we need to compose the letters to include in the packages. We can figure it all out when I sneak into your apartment later."

The idea of her sneaking into his apartment felt damned good to Josh. Not that it was for anything other than her helping him the way she promised. Which he really appreciated.

But he couldn't help recalling those kisses…

Maybe he could work another one or two into their visit tonight. But that would be all. His body's reaction to this sexy and wonderful woman's presence notwithstanding.

Chapter 11

Before Janna could help Josh with his career, she had a job to do—one she really loved. First things first.

When she arrived at the shelter, she noted which staffers were outside and not currently training dogs, and she left Wizzy with Chessie.

Then she checked on Mika, even though Kyle told her that he'd done so a couple of times since he'd arrived an hour earlier.

"That staffer Josh popped in to check on Mika too a little while ago," Kyle added. "Although I bet he also hoped to see you here."

Janna made herself laugh at Kyle's curious expression. No doubt he wanted her to explain the relationship between Josh and her.

Well, there was no relationship. There couldn't be, even if the idea sounded good to her, especially considering who Josh really was. She was a vet tech and always would be, even if she got somewhere with her writing. She most likely would always live in Chance. And he was a best-selling author who wouldn't be around here long if he could help it. They were just friends, and she was going to help the writer-in-hiding maintain his career to the extent she could, which wasn't much. But she could run errands and mail things for him. Carefully, so as not to give any indication of her involvement or his whereabouts.

"Josh seems like a good new staff member," she said. "And I like the way he appears to have taken over being Spike's handler here—not that the former K-9 needs a lot of handling."

"I agree. Anyway, I haven't heard about any other animals here who need our help at the moment. I want to go check on our former patients, Squeegee, Elmer, Pekie and Furball—and also make sure everyone else is doing okay."

This was their norm when they got to the shelter clinic. Of course Kyle was in charge and gave Janna orders as required, but she had a good idea of what needed to be done to follow up with any animal's care.

After Janna checked on Wizzy and Chessie outside—her dog seemed to be having fun—they headed first to the small animal building to check on Furball as well as the other cats. Furball seemed well, coming to the front of his enclosure when he saw the humans and demanding attention by meowing and swatting at the mesh.

The other cats inside also seemed to want attention, but that wasn't what Janna and Kyle were there for. Fortunately, some staff members walked in to remove a couple cats at a time from their enclosures and entertain them with knitted balls and other toys.

"They look good," Kyle told the staffers.

Denise and Bibi, both in matching green shelter T-shirts, smiled. "They seem happy," Denise said.

Leaving the cat house, Janna and Kyle headed to the building for medium-size dogs to check on Squeegee and Elmer. As they drew near, Janna was delighted to see Josh exiting the building with Spike.

She stooped to pet Spike between his ears, then looked up at Josh. "Everything okay in there? We're going to make sure Squeegee and Elmer are doing well." Perfectly normal. She would say that to any staff member. She managed to glance into Josh's face.

He nodded. "As far as I could tell, though I really didn't spend much time inside. I was walking Spike and just stopped in." But his expression suggested he had a lot more to say.

Of course, they couldn't talk about any of it there. She merely said, "Wizzy and I are probably going to hang out here a while longer. Maybe we'll see each other at dinner."

She wished dinner could be in his apartment again. But she suspected that the best way for them to secretly move the packages from her car to Josh's unit was to ask Scott and Nella for more help at dinner in the cafeteria.

Kyle entered the medium dog building ahead of her. There didn't appear to be anything going on that would require her to stay at the shelter overtime today. However, it was late enough that Janna wouldn't be going back to the downtown clinic anyway. It shouldn't matter to Kyle where she spent the rest of that day.

"Yeah, see you later," Josh said in a low voice, then he and Spike continued on their walk while Janna hurried after Kyle.

Of the two dogs she and Kyle wanted to check on,

only Squeegee was there, and he seemed fine. Elmer must be out on a walk with a staffer, a good sign.

They also looked in on the other dogs in the building's enclosures, and all appeared okay, many of them coming up to the mesh and wagging tails, clearly requesting attention and treats. All of that was normal, but as always it tore at Janna's heart.

As at every shelter, the animals there needed and deserved loving homes, not just walks, training and food. She knew that Scott and Nella and the managers always worked hard to show off the resident animals to people who came to meet them—even making staff members remain in their apartments so none would be obvious to the visitors. To the world, they were all formerly homeless people hired to help care for the animals—but in reality each was there under protection from danger in their lives.

Including Josh.

Well, at least Janna could help out as a vet tech, making sure, to the extent she could, that all the animals were well cared for and as healthy as possible. Helping to prepare them for their forever homes.

Janna and Kyle left the building for medium-size dogs and headed for the toy dog building. They looked in on all the pups there as well and spent a bit of time making sure Pekie was doing okay.

Finally, they visited the building for large dogs. Janna was glad to see that the dogs not out for walks there also seemed to be doing fine.

Finishing the late-afternoon routine, Janna retrieved Wizzy from Chessie, who gave a glowing report of how much fun they'd had, as usual. Janna returned with Wizzy to the clinic and took her to a good-size enclosure, giving her treats.

When it was nearly evening, Kyle prepared to head back to the downtown clinic, though Janna's workday was ending.

"Your schedule tomorrow is about the same as today's," he said as he got his things ready to leave. "Coming out to the parking lot with me?"

"I plan to leave soon," she said, "but I'm going to take Wizzy for another walk here, then probably stay for dinner."

"Great. Well, have a good evening, and I'll see you tomorrow."

She walked out with Kyle, Wizzy beside her on his leash. As Kyle aimed for the front gate, making a phone call probably to Nella to let him out, Janna led Wizzy in the other direction.

It was nearly dinnertime, so there weren't many staffers out training dogs, but there were a few. All seemed happy to have Janna and Wizzy still around, and Chessie even invited them to walk with her and Oodles, her dog charge at the moment.

Janna hoped she would see Josh again soon to talk privately about this evening. For now, though, she enjoyed being with Chessie and Oodles and getting a chance to say hi to other staffers.

They drew close to the main buildings—and there he was. Josh, as usual with Spike, came from behind the building for small dogs and started toward them.

Okay, how should she handle this, with all the other staffers around?

"Go see Josh," she told Wizzy, letting go of his leash, and her pup dashed over to him.

Josh knelt to hug Wizzy. "Hey, it's dinnertime, right?" he said, looking at Chessie. "Are you heading to the cafeteria?"

Janna was, though she didn't say so yet.

"Sure," Chessie said. "I was going to take Oodles back to her enclosure now, so I'll see you when I get there."

"How about you, Janna? Will you and Wizzy join us?"

"Sure," she said. Dinner first, then a secret meeting in his apartment.

"Why don't you come with me while I take Spike back to his enclosure?" he asked her. "It won't hurt for a vet tech to walk with us and look him over, just in case."

Oh. That was what he had in mind. "I'd be glad to check on Spike," she said. Fortunately, Chessie was headed to the small dog building with Oodles, a toy poodle mix.

Janna glanced briefly at Josh, then pasted a smile on her face. As they continued on, she actually did observe how the German shepherd walked. He looked normal to her, fortunately. Spike had had an injured leg a while ago, but with veterinary care, he'd healed from that.

"Spike looks fine to me," she said, hoping to get the conversation going.

"I figured he was, but he's certainly a good reason for me to spend time talking to a vet tech." Josh smiled down at her, then seemed to grow serious. "So, here's what I have in mind for tonight. I've already requested that Scott and Nella help us sneak what you've brought to my apartment after dinner, then back down again after we've discussed how to get the packages ready to mail out. For now, we'll meet with them in the cafeteria for dinner, then they'll walk with you to your car, ostensibly to say goodnight and maybe discuss some animals' health. I've already jotted down what the notes to send with the stickers should say, and I've got names and addresses ready for you. Fortunately, since I still have internet access, it wasn't hard to get that together."

"That all sounds fine to me," Janna said.

No other staffers were inside the building for medium-size dogs. Presumably they were all at dinner now, and Josh quickly put Spike into his enclosure, giving him a going-away treat.

"Okay, then. Let's go have dinner—and get things started."

It was fortunate that the director of Chance Animal Shelter was understanding. Josh gathered that Scott was quite versatile in what he did for the staff members. Scott and Nella were kind, protective and used to doing what was needed to keep each staff member, and the others around them, safe.

Though Josh figured he was one of the most unique staffers who'd come to live here under protection. Even though everyone was unique in their own way.

As he walked with Janna and Wizzy toward the cafeteria, Josh kept his pace brisk and his voice low. "I think I have things figured out for this evening. Did you leave the things you picked up in your car?"

"Yes," she said, also quietly, though he was able to hear her. "I have them in generic tote bags, but I didn't want to try to bring them into the clinic since Kyle would be there and might wind up being curious about what they contained. I figured it wouldn't be a good idea to explain—or figure out how to lie in a way that would work."

"Sounds good. Scott's help will make it easier to get them into my apartment and back out again later."

"I hope that's the case," Janna said. "I considered that we could go over everything in the clinic, but even though we keep the doors locked, it's a lot more public than your apartment. Plus, we'd need a good reason for you to be there with me."

"Yeah, this way we'd just need to figure out why you're joining me in my apartment if anyone sees us. Hey, maybe we can share a kiss for them to watch." He looked at Janna and raised his eyebrows suggestively.

Fortunately she laughed.

Even though the idea played games with a certain body part of his…

In the cafeteria, a lot of staff members were apparently ready for dinner. Josh hung back a little. "You go grab a seat near Scott and Nella and leave Wizzy there. I'll get my food and join you, then you can pick up your dinner too. That way it won't be too obvious that we want to eat together."

Janna's glance reminded him yet again that they had several reasons to eat together—and not just because of how she was helping him. Okay, she might not feel as attracted to him as he was to her, but she clearly liked the idea of him as a writing mentor.

And he, surprisingly, liked the idea too—not just because it was a convenient trade for getting his promotional stuff out there.

He was looking forward to seeing what she'd brought, and talking with her about what to print and how to prepare the packages and mail them.

He looked forward to it a lot.

He hoped it would all go as well as he anticipated.

And maybe also in ways beyond just promoting his newest book.

Chapter 12

So Josh thought they'd be hiding the fact they wanted to eat dinner together?

Janna wasn't sure that would be the case, especially since they were entering the cafeteria together. But though she'd gotten the indication a few times that some staffers suspected she and Josh were interested in one another, surely no one knew the real reasons why they were hanging out. No one knew that Janna was looking for help with her writing or that Josh needed help promoting his book.

Even if Janna did feel some attraction, it was going nowhere, no real relationship, at least—though it might in fact be a good cover for what was actually going on, if any staff members were making assumptions. And it surely wouldn't be obvious that she was helping Josh by going to various areas outside the shelter to pick up things he needed.

Or at least not obvious to staff members. Scott and Nella already knew the reality.

"See you at the table," she muttered to Josh. Greeting some of the staffers nearby, such as Chessie, Augie and Bibi, Janna directed Wizzy toward Scott and Nella's table.

"Hey, Wizzy," Nella said almost immediately, standing up from her seat and patting the pup on the head. "Welcome. Would you like to join us to eat tonight?" She looked up at Janna. "Are you staying here for dinner before heading back to town?"

"Sounds good to me. And I'm sure I'll find things Wizzy can eat too."

"Of course." Many seats around Nella were already occupied, including one where Scott had obviously left his things. But there were still two empty seats on Nella's other side. Janna quickly sat down on the farthest one. "I'll go get my meal in a minute," she said.

Nella nodded and smiled without suggesting who might take the other seat. But Janna was sure the shelter's assistant director was on her wavelength.

"So how were things at the shelter clinic today?" Nella asked, most likely just to make conversation. She and Scott would always be informed right away about any animals in distress.

"Just fine," Janna said and proceeded to tell her that Mika was the only animal currently under their care and that she seemed to be improving. She stroked Wizzy's head as her dog sat beside her alertly on the floor. Possibly he was wondering when he'd get some of the food he was definitely aware of with his keen sense of smell.

"Glad everyone seems to be doing well," Nella said, then looked over Janna's shoulder and smiled as Scott sat down next to her. He had a plate of food in one hand and a glass of water in the other.

"Hi, Janna," he said. "Good to see you."

It was definitely good to see him, Janna thought, since the evening would be more difficult if he and Nella weren't able to help her take things to and from her car later.

"If you'd like to go get your dinner now that would be fine," Nella told her. "I'll join you. Scott can save our seats and keep an eye on Wizzy."

"I'd be glad to," Scott agreed, "especially the keeping an eye on Wizzy part. Would it be okay if I gave him a small piece of hamburger?"

Janna laughed. "Why don't you ask him?" She rose and handed Scott Wizzy's leash. She watched, amused, as the director immediately pulled a small piece of meat from his sandwich and handed it to her happy dog.

As Nella and Janna started walking toward the food counter, Josh came toward them, holding a filled plate.

"Hi," Janna said to him. "Looks like we're going to be tablemates since I'm here for dinner tonight. Your seat is near mine." As if Josh wasn't well aware of those things. But in case anyone happened to be listening—and there were quite a few staff members also heading for the tables carrying their dinners—it didn't hurt to be discreet in what she said and how she said it.

Then, ignoring Josh, or at least trying to make it look as if she wasn't totally aware of where he was, Janna followed Nella through the crowd till they reached the food counter.

Janna had eaten at the cafeteria enough to be aware of the usual setup, with salad fixings at one end, followed by sandwiches such as hamburgers, and then whatever entrees were available for dinner plus side dishes. To-night the meal included roast chicken. Janna put some chicken on her plate along with a good-size salad and a small glob of mashed potatoes. She'd share her chicken with Wizzy, being careful not to give him any bones. Her dog had already gotten some beef, thanks to Scott. And she'd give him a healthier meal for dogs, though a small one, when they finally got home.

She got herself some water out of the dispenser, then returned to the table to sit down.

Beside Josh. He was already eating but stood at her approach, clearly a gentleman—even though chivalry wasn't the norm these days. He pulled out her chair, but she didn't immediately sit. After placing her dishes on the table, she retrieved Wizzy's leash from Scott, thanked him and then sat.

Dinner was excellent. Wizzy apparently thought so too since he kept begging for more chicken, but Janna didn't overdo it.

Janna participated in conversation with others around the table about taking care of the animals, but every now and then, she shared glances with Josh. He seemed to finish eating fairly soon. So did she. But they lingered until after most of the others got up and left.

Not Scott or Nella, though.

Eventually, the cafeteria had almost emptied. "Can we walk you to your car?" Nella asked Janna. Clearly the directors were ready to help as Josh had asked.

Josh rose with them. "Good dinner, but I'm heading to my room now. Maybe I'll see you tomorrow."

Or later tonight, Janna thought.

She was glad that no one appeared to be around as she walked outside with Scott and Nella. When they reached her car, she unlocked it after looking around to make sure no one else was in the lot or on the road by the shelter. It all looked empty, fortunately—not that anyone was likely to know what she was up to.

She handed one of the two tote bags to Nella and the other to Scott.

"We'll take these to Josh's apartment right now—surreptitiously," Nella said with a smile. "Then I'll come back to get you. That's what Josh indicated he wanted to happen. Right?"

"Exactly. I'd like to stay there for about an hour, then return to my car with the bags."

"Got it," Scott said. Soon, he and Nella had gone back through the gate, leaving Janna outside with Wizzy.

To make their presence at least a little less obvious, Janna stayed inside the vehicle with her pup, just checking some emails on her phone. Wondering how things were going with Josh getting those bags—and how they'd go when she sneaked back inside to talk to him about it all.

In his apartment, alone, at night…

With Scott or Nella primed to come get her eventually and walk her back to her car, Janna couldn't allow her imagination to go too wild, at least.

She deleted a bunch of spam in her email, then responded to a couple of messages from some friends. Glancing often back at the fence…

There. It finally opened again, and Scott stood there waiting for her.

"Let's go, boy," she said to Wizzy in the back seat, and got out of the car.

It had only been a short while since dinner, so Josh hadn't been waiting in his apartment long. Nevertheless, it felt like forever.

Hopefully no one would see Janna hanging out with Scott or Nella in a way that might seem noteworthy. Most staff members were aware of animals needing special care, and there was only one such dog now. Anyone paying attention would know Mika wasn't doing too badly. Which was of course a good thing. But there wasn't much veterinary reason for Janna and Wizzy to be around this late.

For now, Josh sat on the sofa with the television broadcasting a show he paid no attention to. He wasn't in the mood for news or game shows, so he'd it tuned to a show about saving animals in shelters, though the shelter featured was nothing like this one. But people making sure dogs and cats were well cared for while waiting for their forever homes was nice to have on in the background.

However, this evening he was definitely Nolan Hoffsler, attempting to save his writing career, waiting for help from an aspiring writer who seemed to care about what happened to him. And maybe not just because he could advise her with her own writing. And—

There. He heard a quiet knock on his door and dashed over to open it, then stood back while Janna, Wizzy,

Scott and Nella hurried in. He glanced out to make sure none of his neighbors were in the hallway, then ducked back in and quickly closed the door.

"Good evening again," he said to his visitors, glancing first into Janna's lovely eyes, then down at the large tote bags Scott and Nella were holding. "Thanks for coming." He wasn't sure what was in which bag, but he had told Scott what Janna would be bringing. Still, knowing the director's determination to keep the shelter safe, Scott had probably looked inside to make sure there wasn't anything that might cause any danger.

Envelopes, stationery and stickers were pretty safe, and there would be no return addresses or other indication of the shelter's location. Scott should have no problem with supplies like these.

"You're welcome," Nella said.

"We'll put these down and leave," Scott told them, lowering the bag he held to the floor. "Everyone's in their own apartments now, so Janna's unlikely to be seen, but we'll come back for her in about an hour and see her out."

"That's right," Nolan told them. "Janna and I will go over what I need her to do with the contents, but she will have to print a few things outside the shelter."

"Got it," Scott said.

"Sorry we don't have a printer here you can use," Nella added, also putting her tote bag on the floor. "And too bad we couldn't let you bring one with you. They tend to be bulky, so it'd be hard to sneak it here."

"I'm just glad you let me bring my laptop and access the Wi-Fi here," Nolan said. "I know that's pretty unusual here."

"Definitely." Scott turned toward the door. "We'll let you get started with what you need to do." He opened the door, looked outside, then motioned for Nella to follow.

Nolan was soon alone with Janna in his apartment, along with Wizzy. The thought of being alone with this lovely vet tech immediately sparked something in his body. But anything beyond discussing the task ahead of them just wasn't going to happen.

He carried both tote bags into his small kitchen, placing them on the table. "I'll go get the notes I've been making. Let me say again that I really appreciate all this—what you've done so far and what else you'll be doing." There were no guarantees, of course. But Janna had indicated she was willing to help. Just because.

She was a wonderful human, and not only because of how she treated animals.

"Well, I appreciate the comments you've given me so far about my writing," she said, "and how you'll work with me to improve it. I owe you, and this is a small way to repay you. Besides, I'd hate to see Nolan Hoffsler's career do anything but continue to thrive, so I'm glad to help."

Nolan smiled and began removing things from the bag. She'd done just as she promised, bringing a couple large postal mailers, a lot of smaller envelopes that could be individually addressed, and attractive notepaper that could be printed with an explanatory message for the various booksellers. There were also various stickers with small, attractive borders that he could sign, taking the place of his personal signature.

All looked good.

"Excuse me for a minute." He hurried into his bedroom, where he picked up a spiral notepad. After spending lots of time on the computer, he'd jotted down bookstores he'd visited in the past, including their addresses and the names of their owners or managers.

From the list, Janna should be able to print mailing labels and place them on the smaller envelopes. She'd be in charge of packaging the envelopes with the printed notes and the signed stickers. Hopefully she could print the labels and notes tomorrow. He'd work on signing the stickers tonight and then figure out a way to hand them to her when she came to work at the shelter tomorrow.

It could be time-consuming, but it wasn't that complicated, and as he explained, Janna seemed to catch on immediately. She asked cogent questions and appeared amused at the vast number of booksellers he hoped to reach this way.

"Too bad I can't jump in and introduce myself," she said at one point with a laugh. "After all, I want to be in your shoes someday, out there with bestsellers that people want me to sign. Maybe I'll send signed stickers too when I can't be there in person."

"One of these days," Nolan said, grinning. "Especially with my help with your writing."

"Oh, of course."

Janna helped him return everything to the tote bags, other than the blank stickers.

"The hour isn't up yet," she said to him. "I don't want

to bother Scott or Nella. Is it okay if I hang out here for the next twenty minutes?"

"Definitely," Nolan said. Too bad it wasn't even longer. But for now, he stood and took Janna into his arms.

Wizzy rose, then lay back down again when it became clear that they weren't going anywhere.

"Would enjoy thanking you in a more thorough way," Nolan said against Janna's hot lips, which moved against his. "Maybe someday we'll have more time here alone together, and we can..."

He didn't get to finish.

"Someday," Janna interrupted, and pressed her curvaceous body hard against him. They shared several more kisses until she finally pulled away.

"Almost time for Scott and Nella to arrive." Her tone sounded regretful as she pulled her cell phone from her pocket and looked at it. She seemed to try to compose herself—and that was when Nolan heard the quiet knock they were expecting on the door.

Oh, yes. Maybe someday...

Chapter 13

It was finally time.

Janna had started typing up the labels and notes for the booksellers last night after she got home. She appreciated how easy it was to read Nolan's cursive for everything he wanted her to print out. She'd been able to add the information easily to the computer files she set up.

She still had lots to do today though, including printing everything, then writing letters to both of her sisters to remind them to mail the sealed, labeled and stamped envelopes she would put in the packages to each of them. Hopefully there would be no nosy sneak peeks on their part. She'd need to create mailing labels for those large packages to her sisters as well.

She'd managed to push all of that aside in her mind as she worked at the downtown clinic that morning. She helped care for ailing animals and made sure those who were well stayed well with vaccinations and annual physicals. The usual. Although none of it was really usual, thanks to the many individual pets she and Kyle examined.

But the time had gone fast. She'd finally completed her shift at the downtown clinic and could head to her condo for a couple of hours to work on Nolan's mailing materials. At least she didn't need to finish everything today. She wouldn't get the signed book labels back from him till after her shift at the shelter clinic that afternoon.

"Let's go home for a while," she told Wizzy as they left the downtown clinic and headed to her car.

And now it all was back in her mind. Oh, she felt she'd gotten a reasonable start before, and she wouldn't have to spend a whole lot of time on it now. At least not till she got home again that night with Nolan's signed stickers. She hoped to get everything mailed tomorrow, which meant she might not get much sleep that night.

Well, that was fine. She'd be doing something worthwhile besides sleeping.

Once she reached her condo, she put together a quick tuna fish salad sandwich for her lunch and give Wizzy a snack, too. Then she got busy. And was delighted that things went fairly quickly. In fact, when it was time to head to the shelter, she had things mostly done and organized on her kitchen table.

With luck, she'd be able to finish the printing and address labels and package Nolan's stickers when she returned that evening. She might still get some sleep that night.

No need to bring anything along today, though she'd have stickers to bring back with her later. Then she'd have the fun of organizing them in envelopes.

This certainly wasn't the way she'd anticipated spending time as a veterinary technician and aspiring writer. But she had good reason to do it. And in a way, she was pleased that she was not only be able to help Nolan, but she also had a hand in planning how to help him.

But time to get back to her usual routine now, for a while at least. "Let's go, Wiz," she told her wonderful and patient dog. He'd slept beside her as she worked at the computer.

Soon, they arrived at the shelter for the afternoon.

"How are things going?" Nella asked as she let Janna and Wizzy through the front gate.

Janna was somewhat surprised to see Nella's dark brown hair loose that day. She usually had it fastened behind her head. Maybe she felt less formal today than usual. Not that she ever appeared formal in her Chance Animal Shelter shirt, even though today's had the word *Manager* by the logo on the pocket.

"You mean the stuff I've been working on at home?" Janna felt certain that was what Nella was referring to, but even though no one was nearby, she didn't want to go into detail. "I think it's progressing well."

"Good. But I'm glad you're here, and I'm sure Dr. Kornel will be glad to see you too. The clinic has been busy."

That startled Janna. "What's going on?"

"Oh, we've taken in three more dogs at the shelter. A contact of Scott's asked us to, and since we've got a visit from some potential adopters planned in a few days, we're likely to have more room for them."

They'd reached the hall that led to the clinic. "Do you know if the newbies are okay?" Janna asked.

"That's for you and Dr. Kornel to determine. But we

wouldn't have taken them in if they didn't at least seem healthy."

Janna knew that was the case. Still, it sounded like she would be busy that afternoon.

Somehow, she'd have to get those stickers from Josh, though. Yes, he was Josh in her mind again, a staff member here that she'd need to meet up with. But he simply had to hand over the signed stickers and trust her to get everything right. And she believed he already did.

Wizzy pulled slightly on his leash. Janna had been in such a hurry to get inside the shelter that she hadn't taken her pup for a walk. Now was the time to do so, before she got busy helping with the new arrivals. "Wizzy and I are going out for a minute," she told Nella, then said to her pup, "Okay, boy."

"Sounds good. I'm sure Scott and I will pop in now and then at the clinic to see how things are going."

Janna couldn't help hoping that someone else at the shelter would as well. But she was certain Josh would somehow get the stickers to her before she left for the day. Or night. She might wind up being here for a while, depending on how those dogs were doing.

She was delighted to see that very person walking Spike when she led Wizzy to the central path through the shelter grounds, although Josh was about a building away from them. But he obviously saw her too and headed in their direction. He was wearing a navy blue shelter shirt today.

"Hi," she said as they drew close. "And hi, Spike." Wizzy had already gotten down to business, but that gave Janna a moment to pat the other dog. Then her dog rose to get his greeting from Josh.

"I heard we have some new arrivals here at the clinic," Josh said, "and that Dr. Kornel is already there looking them over. I should be able to pop in and get a glimpse of them."

Josh held her gaze, his deep brown eyes suggesting he wanted to do more than just see the new dogs. But if she was as busy as she anticipated that afternoon, she wasn't sure she'd be able to spare a moment to talk to him anyway.

Maybe another dinner here at the shelter was in order later—but only after the new dogs didn't require any ongoing care that day.

But she needed at least a tiny bit of alone time with him to get those stickers.

"Wizzy and I are going there now. But…well, I'm sure we'll see you later."

Somehow. Somewhere at the shelter.

Too soon, Josh said, "See you later," then began walking away with Spike.

Janna had a ridiculous urge to follow, to somehow remain in his presence. But she had work to do, so she headed back to the clinic with Wizzy. She locked Wizzy into one of the empty enclosures with a dog bed, blanket and water bowl. "Wait here, boy," she said. "I'll be back soon."

She hurried into the locker room and grabbed a clean scrub jacket before heading to the examination rooms.

Kyle was in the first one. A mostly white pit bull mix

was on the table in front of him, and he turned briefly as Janna walked in.

"Oh, good, you're here," he said. "I'm just finishing my initial exam of this girl, and I'll want you to draw a little blood for her tests. Janna, meet Minnie."

Apparently the dog knew her name, since she wriggled beneath Kyle's hands. Janna joined them to pat Minnie, then hurried to the sink to wash her hands and prepare the syringes.

After the blood draw, she helped Kyle get Minnie down from the table, and they took the pup into one of the holding rooms. Mika, still wearing her cone, was in one of the room's enclosures. She looked good to Janna, but as Kyle locked Minnie in a separate enclosure, Janna asked, "How's Mika doing?" She assumed Kyle would already have checked.

"Very well. We should be able to remove the cone tomorrow, and if all's as good as I think, she can go back out to join the rest of the dogs."

"That's great!" Janna said.

They went into the next holding room and got a black French bull mix out of an enclosure there. The paperwork on the nearby table said he was Bambam.

Janna helped examine Bambam and drew some of his blood as well. After they returned Bambam to his enclosure, the examined the third newcomer, a middle-size unknown mix, perhaps part beagle, named Baxter.

"Go ahead and start the blood test analyses," Kyle said when Baxter was back in his enclosure. "I'll go tell Scott that their initial exams seemed fine, but the tests will be the final determination of whether they're well enough to stay here and be trained with the rest of the dogs."

The tests, Janna knew, should reveal any possible anemia, immune deficiencies and other potential internal disorders. They didn't have a full array of tests here, at this small clinic, but if anything abnormal showed up, they could have the blood checked at the downtown clinic.

For now, holding the vials of blood labeled by dog, Janna walked to the lab at the end of the hall as Kyle headed for the exit. She put the tubes into holders, but before she could grab the proper chemicals, she heard what sounded like a knock on the clinic door.

Yes, there'd been some noise; a couple of the dogs barked. Had Kyle returned? Had he forgotten his key?

But when she opened the door, it wasn't Kyle she saw.

Josh, with Spike leashed beside him, stood there. "I saw Dr. Kornel leave," he said. "Can I come in?"

"Of course." Janna stepped aside, and Josh and Spike walked in. She locked the door behind them. "I'm glad to see you here actually. I wasn't sure when we'd have an opportunity to talk. We need to discuss how I can get the signed stickers from you discreetly."

"Exactly," he said. He looked her directly in the eyes, his gaze definitely intense. It was somehow alluring, even though he didn't seem to want to come on to her. Not now, at least. "And I need to talk to you about them a bit. I've written different signatures on some of the stickers and need to go over the list with you again to request that you send them to the right places."

Interesting, Janna thought. What were those differences, and how had he decided which to send where?

Well, this wasn't the time to talk about it. Quickly making a decision, she said, "Looks like I'll be hanging out here for dinner again. And then I'll just happen to show up at your apartment."

"Sounds good," Josh said with a laugh that was way too sexy. "See you at dinner." Then he and Spike left.

Janna went to get Wizzy. Time for them to take a walk. They'd be staying there for a while longer that day.

And yes, Janna would get to see Josh again.

Okay, maybe he was being a bit of a jerk about this, Josh thought as he left the clinic and walked Spike back to the center path.

His mind kept returning to why he wanted to talk to Janna about who to send which stickers to. Dumb, maybe. But last night, alone in his apartment, he had been signing stickers with a regular ballpoint pen when he realized he had something better stashed in the few supplies he'd been able to bring to the shelter.

It was a decorative fountain pen he'd received as a gift from a reader a long time ago, and he'd used it now and then to sign books when on tour. The ink was blue and came out thicker than the black ink from the pen he'd been using.

Well, since he couldn't actually sign books in person, he might as well make his signature look more attractive. And so he'd stopped using the cheap pen and started using the better one, after having gotten maybe half the stickers signed.

Why hadn't he remembered the fountain pen before? It wasn't as if he had a whole lot of stuff from his real life with him now. But Janna had brought him the regular pen along with the stickers, and he'd just started using it without considering the stash of thumb drives or small notebooks—or better pen—that he had managed to bring along.

And the fact that going over the variety of signatures tonight with Janna meant they'd be alone again in his apartment for a short while… Irrelevant, no matter how much he wished he'd be able to make even more use of that alone time. A thank-you kiss would be fine, though.

"Are you doin' okay?" Augie asked, catching up beside him with Oodles. "You and Spike?" The senior never appeared to walk very fast, but he'd hurried somewhat to catch up with Josh and Spike. Yes, Josh again, now that he was out with other staff members here, no matter that his mind had been focused on Nolan signing book stickers—and a bit more.

Josh must look stressed or something. "I'm doing fine," he replied. "In fact, I'm doing great—as I always am when I walk with my buddy Spike." He bent to give the shepherd a quick pat on the head, and Spike seemed to revel in it, looking up at him as if he wanted to smile. "How about you and Oodles?"

According to Augie, they were doing just fine too. Josh and Spike continued to walk with them, joining up for a while with Bibi and Ashy the poodle and Leonard and the black Lab Moe.

Josh made it a point to focus on his work with Spike and his fellow staffers. No sense thinking about any of the other stuff. He'd work out getting Janna to his apartment later, so he could finally hand over the stickers and discuss how best to distribute them. And that was all.

Chessie and Russell, a Jack Russell terrier mix, soon joined them. Josh enjoyed seeing how the other staff members switched dogs often. It was probably good for the dogs' training, and the staffers' abilities, to work with a variety.

On the other hand, he was happy just to walk with Spike when he needed to be out here. Did the others think him odd, inefficient, stupid?

Well, he didn't care—much. And if he stayed here much longer, he'd insist on training some other dogs, which should be enjoyable.

The afternoon wore on. Josh was always pleased to reach the end of the walkway nearest the main buildings, but he never saw Janna or Dr. Kornel outside. He hoped all was well with any animals they were dealing with in the clinic.

When it was nearly dinnertime, he took Spike back to the medium dog building. Then, along with some other staffers, he headed to the cafeteria.

But he didn't see Janna there. Surely, she planned to get the stickers from him somehow, right?

He'd just have to wait for now, though he wished he could sneak away and head into the clinic to find her.

He didn't see Scott or Nella in the cafeteria either, although it was early enough that they might not have arrived yet. Their usual table didn't have anyone sitting at it. The low hum of voices in the room, and a general lack of staff members, also indicated not many people had stopped for dinner this early.

Josh headed to the food counter and selected his dinner—a salad, some meatloaf and mashed potatoes and a side of broccoli. Everything looked and smelled good, and Sara, the cook, was there overseeing it all, as usual.

Scott and Nella came in while he was getting his food and began to fill their plates as well. And finally, when they all sat down together, Josh saw Janna enter the cafeteria with Wizzy.

She was still here! Hopefully, they could work things out so he could turn over the stickers to her after dinner. If they waited till others left, no one should see her going to his apartment with him, even for a short while.

Nella and Scott had started usual conversation with staffers—how was everyone doing and which animals had they worked with that day? Josh got to chime in about how smart Spike was and happy he was to still be working with him. Some of the others goaded him a little about being so stuck on one dog and not being versatile. He defended himself humorously, and the conversation turned into a joke fest of sorts without mentioning he was considering working with other dogs.

Then Janna joined them, her plate filled and her leashed dog at her side. Trading glances with Josh as she sat down beside him, she joined the discussion, also teasing him but admitting she understood. After all, despite all the other animals she treated as a vet tech, Wizzy remained her best friend.

"Oh, and by the way," she said, looking from person to person around the table, "you're going to get some more dogs to work with soon, although you might already know that. We're checking out three newbies. Once their blood tests are back, if all's well, you'll get to train Minnie, Bambam and Baxter." Janna went on to describe the new dogs.

Maybe Josh would get to work with one of them too.

Josh took his time eating and noticed that Janna did too. The others around them were soon done and, after grabbing some cupcakes from the food counter, they all left—except for Scott and Nella.

"Everything okay?" Nella asked Josh, glancing from him to Janna and back.

Josh leaned toward her. "I just need Janna to come to my apartment briefly to pick up the stickers I've signed. I have just one little more request for her before she mails them out."

"Got it," Nella said. "I assume that won't take too long."

"That's right."

"Well, take your time sneaking up to the apartment individually," she said, "like before. You have the labels in bags or whatever so Janna can take them with her easily?"

Josh nodded, glancing toward Janna. Her expression was serious and interested.

"Then just drop me a quick text when you want me to let you out of the shelter, Janna," Nella said. "Okay?"

"Definitely."

Josh rose to leave, nodding briefly at Janna. "I'll be in my unit." He figured she would stay an extra few minutes with Scott and Nella, then head toward his apartment. Maybe she would first go to the apartment reserved for clinic personnel to make sure no one was around before coming to his.

And so he wasn't surprised that he had to wait a little while before hearing a soft knock on his door. He'd sat in a chair in his living room, TV off so he could hear, anticipating Janna's arrival soon. When he heard the knock, he figured it was her.

Janna stepped inside quickly with Wizzy when he opened the door, and he closed it behind her. He noticed she held a large tote bag with a veterinary assistant school logo on it. When she put it on the floor, Wizzy sniffed it, and she let him off his leash.

"All look okay out there?" Josh asked immediately.

"If you mean did I see anyone watching me, the answer is that all was fine out there. I didn't see anyone."

They locked glances, but Josh pulled his gaze away first. He had an urge to kiss her—no surprise there. But Nella had made it clear that Janna shouldn't stay long, and that was appropriate.

"Okay," he said. "I've got the stickers laid out here." He walked over to his kitchen table and showed her the various piles—one that he'd signed with the normal pen and the other with his special pen. "Here's the list of people I want the blue ink signatures to go to. And I'm sorry I'm making this even more complicated, but—"

Janna was already looking at his list. "I get it. There are some really big-name bookstores in big cities on this list."

She was correct, of course. He had gotten to know some owners and managers of the most popular bookstores in many areas of the country, including New York City, Los Angeles, Chicago and San Francisco. Some of those were the ones he'd chosen to get the special stickers.

He went over them with her and found himself describing some of the owners and managers and stories from when he'd gone to their stores for talks and signings. Janna laughed and even gasped at some of what he said, and he found himself holding her hand as he pointed out who was who in his notes. He enjoyed the feel of it as she grasped his hand in return.

When he finally stopped talking and looked down at her, he found her watching him with a wonderful, impressed, caring expression on her face.

He couldn't help leaning down, and suddenly they were in each other's arms, sharing a kiss that was suggestive of many things.

"Janna," he gasped against her mouth. Her sensuous curves pressed against him as he grew hard.

"Hey, how about a tour of your bedroom?" she said softly.

And in moments, he was leading her inside, closing the door gently behind them.

He wasn't sure how things were about to go, but he wouldn't want Wizzy upset if it appeared that he was getting physically close to his owner.

Hopefully with clothes off…

Chapter 14

Bad idea, Janna thought as Nolan led her into his room—notwithstanding the fact it had been her bad idea. Sort of. But her suggestion of a tour of his bedroom had been stimulated by that kiss, their closeness…

In a moment, there they were, door closed behind them. Poor Wizzy would be on his own in the rest of the apartment for a while. She hoped he wouldn't be upset if he happened to hear some noise in here.

Would that happen?

Well, why else were they here?

She glanced around. She hadn't seen Nolan's bedroom when she'd been here before since they'd done all their organizing in the kitchen and living room. She'd visited the bathroom but hadn't continued down the short hall to look into the bedroom, figuring that would be too nosy.

But now—

It was compact, with a queen-size bed, a small dresser and a closet door—pretty much the same as the one assigned to the clinic staff.

But suddenly, she was in Nolan's arms again.

"I assume that you had more than one reason to tour my bedroom," he murmured against her lips, and then he was kissing her hotly. His hands began moving down her back till they reached her bottom, and he pulled her against him even closer.

"Definitely," she managed to say as she kissed him back. Her hands were busy too, grabbing his behind and then moving forward, first stroking his leg and then, stepping back a little, reaching for the bulge at the front of his trousers. She moaned at the feel of it, imagining letting it loose and—

"Janna," Nolan whispered huskily. Guiding her to sit on his bed, he removed her black T-shirt. She smiled as he pulled it over her head, and before she could do the same for him, he pulled his own shirt off.

She loved the look of his muscular chest, but before she could touch it, he reached behind her and removed her bra. In moments she felt his lips on her there.

She groaned, throwing herself into the enjoyment. In moments, neither wore any clothes.

She stroked him as he touched her, and she almost moaned in protest as he pulled his hand away. But when she saw him reach into a drawer in the small table beside the bed and draw out a condom, she nodded.

"Good idea," she said, taking it from him. She opened it and rolled it onto his erection. More touching, more kissing, and Janna had never known such exquisite delight.

"This is the best bedroom tour I've ever had," she gasped, and after a short while, she felt herself go over the edge, even as Nolan gasped her name.

They lay there together for a while after that. Janna

felt Nolan gently running a hand over her buttocks as she stroked his back.

This was amazing. Could they do it again?

But then she came to her senses, at least a little. "I didn't anticipate this," she sort of lied. She'd hoped for it but didn't imagine it could be for real. "I wish I could stay here all night. But if I don't text Nella soon—"

"Yeah," he whispered against her ear, and then bit it gently. "I was thinking the same thing. We'd better get up."

And then she would leave. Go home to her condo in downtown Chance, where she'd have to get busy preparing the envelopes so she could mail them tomorrow.

The reminder that she had a job to do for him caused doubt to cloud her thoughts.

She had to ask, though she tried to sound joking. "I really enjoyed what…what we just did. Was that your way of thanking me for doing your mailing for you? If so, guess I'll need to mail a lot more."

His body seemed to freeze up against her. "Is that what you think?" His tone sounded angry, which hurt. But if he had actually believed he was paying for what she was doing for him…

"Not really." She still hoped for his answer, though.

"I'm attracted to you, damn it, Janna." He pulled away and glared at her—and she couldn't help scanning his hard, gorgeous male body as he did. "This wasn't the best idea, but I wanted it and damn enjoyed it. We may never get the opportunity again. But if we ever do—"

"I'd like to do it again too," she whispered, knowing it was true, and pulled him close once more.

But after a long but softer kiss, while she reveled once more in the feel of his hot, hard body against her, she pulled away. "Guess I'd better get dressed," she said regretfully.

She stood up near the bed and put her underwear back on, watching as Nolan did the same. They finished dressing—she was sort of sad when his shorts hid what was underneath—and she hurried to the bedroom door. She'd heard some scratching on it from time to time and figured Wizzy had waited right there.

Sure enough, he soon darted inside the bedroom and sat beside her, waiting for pets.

"All's fine, boy," she said, enjoying the feel of his warm fur.

She followed Nolan back to his kitchen, where they went over his notes for the stickers one last time. She felt confident she could handle everything just as he wanted once she returned home and got started.

Payback or not, she wished she could join him in bed again, but she had things to do for him. She couldn't just hang out here now.

It was time for her to leave. She texted Nella to meet her at the exit gate. Then Nolan and she shared one more heated kiss "See you tomorrow?" he asked.

"Definitely sometime. But I'm going to be busy driving to some post offices once my downtown clinic shift is over."

"Got it. I wonder why."

Janna laughed, then kissed him briefly again. "And whether or not what we did was a thank-you from you, I'm thanking you now for that wonderful experience."

He grinned, then went out into the hallway first to check for anyone around. Fortunately, the hall was empty, so Janna, now with all the stickers and Nolan's notes in her vet assistant school tote, sneaked away and down the stairs.

Missing Nolan already.

Realizing that had to have been a once-in-a-lifetime experience.

After closing the door and locking it when Janna and Wizzy left, Nolan placed his head against its hard surface and just stood there for a long minute.

Wow. That was phenomenal.

Not that he hadn't had good sex before, but Janna was special. Very special. And not just because she was smart and helpful to someone in need. She was the type of person he'd thought only existed in his imagination, a perfect woman who could be a protagonist in one of his books, or the protagonist's significant other.

But she surely couldn't be *his* significant other. Not unless things really changed, and he got his life back. And he didn't worry about endangering her because she was in his presence.

He went into his kitchen. Got a glass of water.

Tried not to think—much—about what he had just experienced. The feel of that warm, curvaceous body under his exploring hands. And what it had felt like when things had gone even further—

Okay, enough. He knew a good way to move his thoughts in another direction: get on his computer.

He wished he'd been working on a story, but with all

the distractions in his life, his real purpose had been put on hold. But he could do other productive things: check his emails. Respond to those from his professional contacts and his fans. That always took a good amount of time and tended to be enjoyable.

Unless more threats appeared there...

He set up his laptop on the kitchen table and got into his emails.

One of the first he saw was from Bruce Ashcourt, his agent. He had visited Bruce in his office in New York City several times and had liked what he had seen of the agency and Bruce's assistants there. Bruce was definitely good at what he did, and he'd surrounded himself with others who also did a great job of selling stories. Nolan kind of wished he could head there now, although that was just another result of wanting to get out of this shelter.

Unless he was able to get together with Janna again as before...

Forget that.

As if he'd ever forget it.

Now, Bruce sounded a bit annoyed. He'd already gotten word from Nolan not to call him, but he was not happy that Nolan hadn't called *him*. He understood that Nolan was keeping quiet somewhere after those threats, but he said they had things to discuss that would work out better if they could talk, even if just on the phone.

But Nolan no longer had his old phone, and even if he did have it, he wouldn't call Bruce. He didn't believe whoever was threatening him was anywhere near his agent or able to capture information from his calls, but there was no sense taking any chances. Especially since some of those threats against Nolan had also been sent to Bruce.

He spent a little time drafting a response that he hoped sounded glad to hear from him and also eager to get back to his writing. He imagined that was what his agent hoped for, even though it was a bit of an exaggeration for the moment.

He did wonder what Bruce had on his mind that necessitated a phone call about, but if it was important, the agent could always explain more in his response email.

Nolan scrolled though the remaining emails. He recognized some fan addresses and clicked on a couple to respond, mostly to say hi back and stay relatable. He didn't open any whose addresses didn't look familiar, in case they included threats. He wasn't in the mood to see those now.

Not that he ever was.

Near the end of the list, Roger Meltry's address appeared. His publicist. Well, he'd have something good to tell Roger soon. Nolan had already hinted at a plan for getting signed books out there without appearing in person, but it would be best not to let Roger know about the stickers till he got confirmation from Janna that she'd mailed them.

Janna. His mind started moving in that direction again. To stop that, he opened Roger's email quickly.

Sure enough, his publicist sounded irritated. Nolan considered not responding at all, not till he had something good to say.

Still, he sent a response that hopefully sounded understanding—yes, more publicity about his latest novel would be a really good thing, and he did have something in the works. Nothing specific, though.

He did open some unfamiliar emails then. None seemed to be from whoever had been threatening him, fortunately. He thought back on all that happened, the fire and gunshot, and the fact that some of his professional team members—like Bruce and Roger—had also received emails that threatened him in really nasty ways. And there'd also been those social media threats.

But he still needed to know whether he could return to his real life.

Okay, he *would* return to his real life—but when?

Right now, he needed to continue to deal with his current situation. He sat a bit longer at the computer, working on an idea for a sequel to *Murder for Dinner*. Although maybe it should be a stand-alone. His mind was always churning away on something to write.

But he found himself thinking about Janna's story as well. How else could he help her to improve it? He typed up and saved a few notes for her. He watched a little nighttime news, then went to bed and thought about Janna's story some more.

He also thought about Janna some more, what she'd be doing for him tomorrow—and what they had done together earlier.

He felt his body react.

He couldn't help but think about seeing her again tomorrow. To find out how things went with her mailing his packages, of course. Could they manage some more alone time?

He could always dream.

Chapter 15

It was midafternoon the next day by the time Janna was able to head to the shelter clinic. She'd been up late getting the envelopes nearly ready to mail, going through Nolan's notes carefully, sorting out which signature stickers needed to be sent to whom and making sure the envelopes she'd already prepared were correct and contained the appropriate stickers.

She didn't seal or stamp them but waited till after her morning shift at the downtown clinic. Returning home, she went over everything again, making sure the right envelopes were enclosed in the larger packages to mail to her sisters.

She loaded the packages into her car and drove with Wizzy first to one nearby town and mailed one of the packages to April. Then, after looking around to try to assure herself no one was paying any attention to her, she drove to another town's post office, farther away, and mailed the other package to Chloe.

"Done," she said when she returned to her car with Wizzy the second time, strapping her pup carefully into the back seat again. She smiled and gripped the steering wheel, wishing she could speak to Nolan now. She should be able to let him know what she'd done in a little while, at least.

Hopefully quietly, although she knew better than to assume they'd get any privacy again that day. Certainly no time as private—and wonderful—as yesterday.

The drive to the shelter clinic was of course longer than usual, but soon Janna was texting Nella, who let her and Wizzy in quickly.

Janna had to brag a little as they entered. "I just did what… I'd been requested to do." She didn't mention Nolan's name, or even Josh's, but she felt sure Nella would know what she was talking about, even if she wasn't aware of the details.

"That's great!" the assistant director said. "So now you're a lot more than a veterinary technician around here, which is great in itself. You do other good deeds as well."

Janna basked in her congratulatory smile a bit—even as she thought about what else she did besides being a vet tech. She wasn't about to mention her writing now. Probably not ever, especially since if Nella or Scott ever learned she did some writing too, they might assume she just wanted to copy what their newest staffer actually did for a living. Never mind that she'd started writing before she even met him.

"I always like helping people," was all Janna said. "And animals too, of course."

They'd reached the central path of the shelter grounds, and Janna was delighted to see that, among other dogs being cared for by staffers, Squeegee was out for a walk with Bibi. The pup was healing pretty well, and staff members had been advised it was okay to walk and train him again but to keep an eye on his reactions. She trusted Bibi to do a good job. And at the moment, she didn't see Squeegee limping at all.

"I intended to peek in on Squeegee later today," Janna said to Nella, "and I still will, but I'm glad to see he's out and about this afternoon."

"Yes, I gather that he's doing well," Nella replied. "That's another thing we can thank you for."

"Just doing my job," Janna said, although she smiled. "I'm really glad he's been healing." She hesitated. "I'll let Josh know all's in order when I see him here later. If I see him. I just wish I could communicate with him by phone or something, like at night, to make it easier."

She wished she could do more with him at night too, but she wasn't about to let Nella know that.

But she'd been thinking about how best to talk to Josh in a secret way when they couldn't be seen hanging out together—and stoking the staff members' assumptions about them. She knew Josh had a computer, so emails might work if she could get his address, but she'd like to talk with him.

"No," Nella told her now. "That could lead to too many difficulties—like his location being found by GPS."

"I figured," Janna said.

After Nella headed back to the office building, Janna walked Wizzy a little more, wanting to make sure all was well before going to the clinic.

And there, as she'd hoped, was Josh, walking Spike a little distance down the path, across from her.

It wasn't a good idea to speak with him directly, but fortunately other staff members with dogs were around. Janna walked toward them, saying hi first to Augie with Russell and then to Veronica, walking Moe. Then she waved toward Josh. "Hi," she said as he drew closer to her—but not too close.

He smiled, but the expression on his handsome face seemed quizzical.

She smiled back and nodded briefly. They'd need to talk later. Maybe they'd find a way to get alone together for a short while when no one was aware of it.

Too bad it was unlikely to be in Josh's apartment.

But all she really needed to do was let him know everything had been packed and mailed the way he wanted. Everything now was out in the wilds of post office land. The packages should start arriving at her sisters' places tomorrow, or maybe a day after. The stickers would soon reach their final destinations.

But Janna wouldn't have to explain any of that to Josh.

For now, she needed to get to the shelter clinic to let Kyle know she was there and get any instructions from him about taking care of Mika and the other animals who'd arrived recently.

"Let's go, Wiz," she told her pup.

Janna used her key to enter the clinic, and Kyle called, "That you, Janna?" He was probably in an exam room.

"Yes, I'm here," she responded. "I'll put Wizzy into one of the enclosures and join you."

It turned out that Kyle was in his office. He looked up from where he sat at his desk with a glare. "I know you said you'd be here late today, but this is even later than I anticipated."

"Sorry." She wished she could give a good excuse, but she wasn't about to tell him she had been on a secret assignment for the writer Nolan Hoffsler, who happened to be a staffer here. "I just had some family matters to attend to." Which was sort of true, since she'd mailed the outer packages to her sisters.

"I understand. I've got family too." His expression warmed a little, and Janna wanted to thank him for his understanding. But better that she just get busy.

"How are Mika, Minnie, Baxter and Bambam? Do we have any other patients?"

"They all seem to be doing well. We got the results of the blood tests, by the way, and nothing bad showed up."

"So glad to hear that." Janna felt relieved as she always did when things sounded good about any of their patients.

"But one of the other shelter cats is here now because of some lethargy. I've already taken a blood test."

"Hope that one turns out well too," Janna said.

Kyle put her to work playing a little with their patients to keep them occupied and monitor their health.

At five o'clock, Kyle popped in on where she was throwing a ball gently for pit bull Baxter to fetch and bring back.

"I'm leaving," Kyle said. "You don't need to stay much longer either, but I assume I'll see you the regular time downtown tomorrow, right?"

"Definitely." She didn't have any further assignments from Nolan, after all.

Nolan. How was she going to speak with him now? She needed to let him know how things went with the mail before she left for the day.

Well, she could always stay again for dinner in the cafeteria.

For now, she led Baxter to his enclosure, gave him a treat and locked him in, then followed Kyle down the hall and watched him leave the clinic.

Next, she looked in on their newest patient, the cat named Gidget, who was fluffy and gray—and sleepy. But she meowed when Janna petted her, and nothing seemed amiss but that sleepiness. Kyle had said he'd taken a blood test, so there was nothing else Janna could do at that moment. While neither Kyle nor she would be around later tonight, Scott or Nella would either peek in on the clinic patients or have staffers do it.

Janna decided to wait a few minutes before heading to the cafeteria where she would hopefully see Nolan. For now, she just headed to Wizzy's enclosure. "Hi, guy." She stooped to give him a hug, then heard a knock on the clinic door.

Someone bringing in a new patient?

But when she answered it, Nolan stood there. She waved him in and shut the door behind him.

"Oh, good," she said. "I was wondering if I should hang around for dinner, but I can tell you right now that everything went fine with mailing things."

"Glad to hear that." Nolan reached out and took Janna into his arms.

Oh, but that felt good. So did his lips on hers...but she couldn't allow herself to get too involved in the moment. They couldn't do anything about it here. And she wasn't about to dash up to his apartment with him— not right now.

But she definitely enjoyed the kiss for a bit longer before taking Nolan's hand and sitting down with him in the waiting room. She described first where she'd taken the packages to mail, and then how she'd filled them the way they'd discussed.

"I can't thank you enough," Nolan said, standing again and reaching for her hand. She stood too, and they kissed once more.

Janna stepped back and regarded his handsome and all too sexy face. "I guess it's time for me to leave the clinic, although I could join you for dinner in the cafeteria tonight. And maybe after—"

He laughed, a sound as sexy as his face. "I recognize I had a once-in-a-lifetime experience with you the other day. And as much as I'd like to do it again, it wouldn't be a good idea for tonight. Although maybe someday—"

"Maybe someday," she couldn't help agreeing, even though she suspected someday would never come.

Time for Janna to go home.

They kissed once more, and with Wizzy, she left the clinic.

Maybe someday.

Josh thought about Janna as he ate at the cafeteria and chatted with the other staffers.

Such a kind, wonderful, helpful and damned sexy woman. But she'd indicated she was leaving for the day, so he didn't see her at dinner, let alone afterward.

He did see Scott briefly though, with no other staffers around, just outside the cafeteria. "Nella told me that Janna would like to communicate with you by phone," Scott said. "Though she did let Janna know you couldn't keep one."

"I understand," Josh said. "I'd like to exchange email addresses with her though, if that's okay, to discuss more about the animals." Was that a good enough excuse?

"Not necessary, since you see her here. It's already unusual for a staff member to be able to email anyone, and I'd prefer limiting it away from the shelter for further security reasons."

And though Josh didn't agree, he figured that was another thing he had to obey around the shelter.

That night, at his apartment, he checked his emails. Publicist Roger remained peeved, again asking when Nolan might be available for public appearances—and yes, he understood why he remained in hiding after those threats, but—

Well, that *but* remained Nolan's way of life now. But he did notify Roger about the latest news: some of their favorite booksellers would get signature stickers in the mail within the next few days. Nolan hoped that would make Roger feel at least a little better.

Apparently it did. When Nolan awoke the next morning and did his usual brief check of email, there was a message from Roger thanking him and sounding pleased. Although public appearances would be way better, and no doubt result in even more book sales.

Nolan understood that. And he was eager to return to reality too. But he hadn't heard anything from the authorities and couldn't be sure that whoever had been threatening him was through. Would leave him alone.

Would leave him alive.

So for now, this remained his reality.

His *maybe someday* wasn't that day either, though. Oh, he saw Janna in the late morning, apparently not long after she arrived. She came out on the shelter's center path with Wizzy while he, as usual, was walking Spike, with quite a few other staffers around. They said hi, she patted Spike while he patted Wizzy, and that was that.

And he saw her again later, when he dropped by the clinic to ask her a few unnecessary questions about Spike's health. He fortunately caught her while Dr. Kornel was in an exam room.

"Everything okay?" she asked him quietly yet urgently. She wore her blue scrubs. He wasn't sure how she could make scrubs look sexy, but she did. Not that it mattered.

"Far as I know," he whispered. "I alerted my publicist to the fact the stickers have been mailed, and he sounded happy about it. I'm sure he'll follow up on it." He paused. "Thanks again for taking care of all that." He looked deeply into her luscious green eyes and wished he could at least kiss her now—but he heard a noise from the exam room where the veterinarian was and figured it wouldn't be a good idea.

"I imagine it'll take a little while before the stores start receiving them," Janna pointed out, "since my sisters have to receive the packages and mail them out."

"That's okay. Just keep me informed."

Nolan didn't mention the idea of them engaging in phone calls—let alone finding a way to get together alone here, in his apartment.

As the door to the exam room started to open, he loudly thanked Janna for her advice about Spike and left the clinic with the pup.

The day seemed to go slowly after that. What next? Would he hear eventually from any of the booksellers about their receipt of the stickers?

He tried not to worry about it, without much success. He spent his time as usual walking around the shelter with Spike, working on training him—as if the smart dog needed it. Interacting with other staff members as they also worked with other dogs.

He wished he could just go into the clinic and visit with Janna and whatever animals she was caring for. Nothing sexy or anything like that. No matter how good it sounded.

He knew he was thinking too much about something that really didn't matter—much. The booksellers would get the stickers eventually. Maybe they'd help sell more books. His name would be out there again, even if *he* wasn't out there again.

This was all nuts—that the focus of his life at the moment depended on the arrival, and utility, of signed stickers.

He needed his real life back.

Right or wrong, he headed to the clinic just before dinnertime. His excuse would be that Spike seemed to be limping a bit, which was a lie. But just in case anyone asked…

As he entered the hallway leading to the clinic, he was glad to see that Dr. Kornel was headed the other direction. Leaving? He soon went out the far door.

But as Nolan reached the clinic door, it opened—and Janna was there with Wizzy leashed beside her.

She smiled as she saw him and gestured for him to come inside. "Everything okay?" she asked.

"As far as I know. But…" Okay, he'd be honest. Somewhat. "But I was hoping to see you again today."

"I was hoping to see you too, but I need to get back to the downtown clinic. A bunch of us vet techs are meeting for dinner. But—"

She dropped Wizzy's leash, and he dropped Spike's, and they kissed. Long and hard and—well, his body certainly reacted.

But she soon pulled away. "So, hi and have a good evening," she said. "I'll be back tomorrow."

Too bad they probably wouldn't spend more time together then either. But he said, "I'll look forward to it."

Then, after another quick—much too quick—kiss, he gave Wizzy a pat, and Janna ushered Spike and him out.

Nolan returned Spike to his enclosure for the night, figuring that Janna would soon leave the shelter with Wizzy. Nolan—no, Josh—was glad it was dinnertime. He'd be able to chat with other staffers and hopefully stop thinking too much about what was, or wasn't, going on with his life.

Dinner wasn't anything too exciting, and neither were his conversations with other staffers. He didn't even try to get together with Scott or Nella. Why bother?

He said goodnight to the few people he'd been sitting with, then headed to his apartment.

Okay, he could do his usual thing here and check his emails.

He had quite a few—and was really happy that a couple were, yes, from some booksellers he knew. Surprisingly, some of his stickers had been received already—maybe in areas where Janna's sisters lived—and they were thanking him. And, at the same time, requesting that he actually visit their stores.

He figured he'd reply tomorrow after pondering the best way to thank them but tell them he was unfortunately too swamped to do what they asked. And what he wanted.

Soon, he'd had enough of the computer. He watched a stupid sitcom on TV and finally went to bed—and recalled all too well how it had felt to be there with Janna...

In the morning he briefly looked at his emails again. One was from Roger. Had the publicist heard from some of the booksellers too?

Nolan opened it to see.

Sure enough, Roger sounded pleased—somewhat. He had heard from just a couple of booksellers who'd received the stickers already, probably the same ones Nolan had received emails from too.

They sounded really happy to have gotten those stickers, Roger said, but they still wanted to know when you'll start appearing publicly again, preferably at their stores. They asked me why you weren't out there now the way you used to be, whether you were sick or something. I haven't responded yet, but I'm not about to tell them the truth, that you're hiding somewhere. I'll maybe even hint that your health is keeping you home or something.

Nolan clasped his fists together before opening them and typing in a reply, thanking Roger for his discretion. I'm hoping things will improve soon, he said, and he certainly did. But meanwhile, it's good to keep the booksellers as happy as possible under the circumstances, and what you're suggesting sounds fine.

Sort of.

He had an urge to ask whether Roger had received any more threats against Nolan. He hadn't received any himself lately, and the most recent had gone to Roger and Bruce. Nolan wondered yet again if whoever it was had gotten tired of the game and wasn't going to threaten him again—let alone carry through and try to harm him.

But if he made that assumption and just left, who knew what would happen?

Maybe the threats had stopped because the person was hoping he'd have exactly that reaction and reappear—so they could kill him.

Enough. He sent his email to Roger and scanned through the rest of his communications. He'd already looked at all the emails from the booksellers he recognized, and there weren't many of them. Not many would have received the stickers yet.

Okay. It was late. Time for bed.

Too bad he'd still be there alone, thinking about, but not with, Janna. How would he sleep that night?

* * *

Not badly, it turned out.

He did his usual thing in the morning of checking his emails before heading to breakfast. Not that he anticipated hearing from more booksellers yet. And not all those on his list would even have his email address, let alone decide to thank him.

Still, there were a few new emails, mostly spam but a couple from writers' organizations he belonged to and, happily, a new one from a fan.

He'd wait till later to respond to that one. He showered, dressed and left his apartment to face the day at the shelter.

Nothing new and exciting there either. He only got a glimpse of Janna in the late morning while he was walking Spike. She was talking to Nella outside the clinic building.

He didn't get any communication with her though. Not a wave or even a smile.

Another day at the shelter, doing the usual. It was Sunday, so no booksellers would receive any stickers in the mail today. Would Janna visit the clinic?

Not only was she there, but she and Wizzy actually stayed for dinner. Nolan was delighted to see her but had to behave like any other staff member, working with Spike, then taking him back to his enclosure and finding a seat near Janna at dinner.

She looked at him quizzically now and then, and they chatted a little, with everyone else around, about how the animals were doing at the clinic.

He said he'd like to visit, and she did manage to take him there after dinner—but a couple of other staff members joined them, including Chessie and Bibi, who seemed delighted to check on the few animals being cared for.

So, no alone time with Janna. Not a surprise. He managed to say goodbye to her when she and Wizzy left. But there wasn't really anything else he could tell her that day about the stickers, even if they'd gotten a couple of minutes on their own. Which they hadn't.

Nothing exciting in his email that night either, which again wasn't a surprise.

It took him a while to fall asleep that night. He kept wondering when it would be okay for him to leave the shelter, as he often did.

And he thought about having Janna in bed with him for other reasons than sleep.

The next day was Monday. Same old, same old these days. Josh acted as he should as a staffer, again hanging out with Spike and other staff members.

At breakfast, Scott stood up and said that they had some potential adopters coming in that afternoon, so everyone needed to stay in their apartments so as not to be seen.

Josh figured Janna might be on duty at the vet clinic then. Too bad she couldn't join him. But her absence from the clinic, and presence with him, would undoubtedly be too obvious.

Besides, other than exchanging friendly greetings and brief discussions on how the animals at the clinic were doing—all well, fortunately, and most were soon to be returned to their usual shelter areas—he didn't really have any interaction with Janna.

A damned shame. And just another reason to want to get out of there and return to his real life.

After all, there'd been no further threats. Maybe whoever was behind them was biding their time, waiting for him to mess up—to reveal his location. He had to be careful.

He cared for Spike again after breakfast, then took his best friend at the shelter back to his enclosure before grabbing lunch in the cafeteria with other staffers. The norm.

The boring, frustrating norm.

Well, Josh would become Nolan again in his apartment later that afternoon, as he usually did when he was there. At least he could get on the computer and check emails yet again. And hopefully work on the new story idea festering in his mind.

He could become himself for a while at least in that way.

Nella was standing at the cafeteria door as he walked out with Augie and Jerry, the guys he'd been sitting closest to at lunch that day. "Hi, guys," she said. "I assume you're heading for your apartments. Please stay there till dinner today."

"Fine with me," Josh said. "I hope you get a lot of our animal residents adopted."

"Me too," said Augie, and Jerry agreed.

"I definitely hope you're right," Nella said.

Josh walked into the apartment building with the others, wishing he could slip away and quickly visit the clinic just in case Janna was there. But of course he couldn't.

Soon, he was alone in the small apartment he currently called home.

"Okay," he said aloud, since he was the only one there he could talk to. "Let's have some fun this afternoon." He looked at the kitchen table where his laptop sat closed. "Yeah, right."

He got into the file for his story idea first, jotting down some more thoughts he'd had and what he still needed to come up with to make it a good thriller. That would take a while, but it was who he was.

Lots more to work on. Lots more to come.

Finally it was time to get into his emails.

He had quite a few new ones, but the first he opened was from Bruce. He was curious what his agent wanted—maybe to press him for more stories. Well, he'd at least be able to tell Bruce he was working on a new idea.

Only—the email wasn't at all what he'd expected.

What Bruce had to say was horrifying.

Where the hell are you, Nolan?

Oh, I know you sent out those stickers to pretend you were signing books. A lot of people know about that now. But let me tell you about the email I just received, from an unknown address, and I haven't been able to track it down.

But it says that, if I'm communicating with you, I'm supposed to let you know that if you don't reappear this Friday at that Great Meals Restaurant that was the source for your damn book Murder for Dinner, the remaining owner will be murdered like the first one was—and not fictionally.

Nolan had written that book in the hopes it would somehow spur the authorities to find the culprit in that homicide. Which they apparently still hadn't. And now someone else was quite possibly in danger of having the same thing happen again.

Unless Nolan appeared when he'd been told.

He had to do something to alert those authorities, just in case. How could he contact them from here? Emailing didn't make sense, but that was his only way to contact anyone outside here.

What should he do? Let undercover cop Scott know? Of course. Should he actually appear at that restaurant? And—

He was startled by a soft knock at his apartment door.

Surely it wasn't the person threatening him. They couldn't be inside the shelter.

He wished he had some kind of weapon to protect himself, just in case. But assuming he wasn't just imagining that knock, he had to go see who it was. He wished he at least had his phone, even if he couldn't make calls, so he could at least take a picture of whoever it was before he got killed…and almost laughed at himself.

Almost. Although maybe he should bring a kitchen knife, even though none of them had any particularly sharp blades.

He stood up from the table and headed for the door.

He knew better than to call out for whoever it was to identify themselves. He didn't want to call attention to what was going on, to let neighbors know he had a visitor.

Taking a deep breath, he quickly pulled open the door.

And gasped. Maybe even smiled a little, if that was even possible at the moment.

"Janna," he said, opening the door a little farther. She was alone, no Wizzy with her, and she hurried inside. He closed the door once more.

But before he could ask what she was doing there, she said, "Oh my, Nolan. What's wrong?"

Chapter 16

Janna had recognized that coming here this late, un-announced, could be a mistake. But she'd wanted to have more time to talk with Nolan about those damned stickers and how they were doing out in the world, as-suming he'd heard anything yet. Even just a few more minutes to discuss it.

Or at least that was her main excuse to herself.

But was it enough of a mistake to engender that look of fury on Nolan's handsome face?

His expression suggested something terrible. And he didn't tell her to leave.

To the contrary, he grabbed her arm, pulled her in-side and closed the door firmly but softly behind her.

"What are you doing here?" he asked through clenched teeth.

She might as well be honest, even though she had an urge to stomp on his foot and run out. "We really haven't had a chance to talk much since I mailed all those stickers for you. They've probably at least started to ar-rive at some of their destinations, and I wanted to know what you'd heard, what the booksellers' reactions were, whether the stickers are helping you sell books and—"

He'd been staring at her as if attempting to read her thoughts from her face. The emotions on his face had changed, or so she believed. Was he really angry?

Was he, for some reason, afraid?

She didn't really know Nolan Hoffsler well enough to be able to interpret his expressions. And now—

His current expression softened. Suddenly, she was in his arms, and he was kissing her. Hard. No tongue action, though. It was enticing, sure—but not entirely sexy. It seemed more as if he was trying to erase what he'd been thinking by kissing her this way.

Or was her imagination taking over reality? She sometimes liked when that happened, when she was attempting to plot a story—but not now.

Before she could pull away though, he did. "Good to see you, Janna," he said. "What are you really doing here?"

She almost laughed. "I just told you. We've barely seen each other over the past couple of days. I debated whether to come to your apartment, but I figured it was the only way to really get a few minutes alone. Which we are, I assume. But I realize now that coming here is a big mistake."

"Why would you say that?"

"Because…because you're acting strange. Oh, not the kissing—that was fun, as usual—sort of. But there's something wrong, isn't there? The way you look, your expression, your body language…" Whether or not she was right, she had to ask, "So what is it? What's wrong, Nolan?"

While they were alone, and while he was most likely

being himself, he was indeed Nolan. But would he respond?

Still facing her in his small living room, he closed his eyes and shook his head. "You won't believe it. Or maybe you will. But I have no idea what I should—" He stopped, then took her hand. "Too bad I don't have any beer here or anything alcoholic. Maybe it would help. But I'll get us both glasses of water. Let's sit down at the table, and I'll tell you. And let me warn you in advance, it's not fun."

"I figured," she said dryly, but she followed him into the kitchen and sat down. She watched as he poured glasses of water, then placed the glasses on the table and sat down beside her.

"Okay, I'll tell you because I don't know what to do. If I leave here now, under these circumstances, I have a feeling I'll learn very quickly why I should stay here. But I can't let that SOB, whoever it is—"

Janna had watched his face, pale and furious, grow even angrier, even though there was a hint of resignation in his expression.

What was going on? Was he deciding to leave here despite whatever danger he was in? Let whatever threats he'd been receiving come true?

"Tell me," she urged softly but firmly.

He took a sip of water, closed his eyes and sighed as he opened them again. "Okay," he said. "The answer to your first question is yes, at least some of the stickers have arrived at their destinations. I've been checking my emails—and I know you're aware I'm allowed to do that despite other staffers being unable to contact the outside world at all."

"Yes, I know that," she said. "It helped you decide to send those stickers out and who to send them to."

"Exactly. Well, I've remained in touch with some of my outside advisors including my publicist, who I told about those stickers. He's gotten some correspondence from the booksellers who've already received some, and so have I."

"That's good, isn't it?" Janna asked.

"Yeah, especially because he's been the one pressuring me the most to start doing talks and signings. But he also knows about the threats, so he seems to understand why, for now, I'm in hiding." Nolan winced.

"Not exactly in hiding," she contradicted, hoping to make him feel a little better. "You're being smart, staying out of sight for a while till the threats against you stop."

His laugh was sharp, not humorous at all. "Yeah, the threats against *me*," he emphasized. "I've been feeling safe here, sure. Maybe a bit stupid, a coward who isn't out there and—"

"You're not a coward," she interrupted. "Not at all. Like I said, you're just smart."

"Well, I need to be even smarter now. You see, my other main advisor, my agent, is aware of those stickers too. And that I'm in hiding. And I got an email from him today that…that is really upsetting. But—"

She could tell that even thinking about it was horrible for him. Maybe it would be better if he didn't try to describe it to her. "Could you show it to me?" she asked.

"I don't think you want to see it," he responded sharply.

But it was affecting him deeply. Badly. And she had really come to care about this man, not just because he was Nolan Hoffsler or that he had started advising her about her writing.

Their kisses and more. His fun with dogs. His... Okay, she didn't have to define everything that attracted her to him. Instead, she responded just as sharply, "Oh yes, I do. Show it to me." She made it a command this time.

Would he?

"You'll probably be sorry. I am. And now I have to figure out how I'm going to handle it."

Still, he stood and reached for his laptop on the kitchen counter. He pulled up a screen. "Here it is." He slid the laptop toward her.

And even expecting something terrible, she heard herself gasp. She wrapped her arms around herself as she focused on what it said:

If you don't reappear this Friday at the restaurant that was the source idea for your damn book Murder for Dinner, the remaining owner will be murdered like the first one was.

"Oh no," she said. "Your agent received this and sent it to you?"

He nodded brusquely. "Today is Monday. That gives me a few days to get out of here and show up there—and decide what to do."

"You don't mean you're actually going to go there,"

Janna said, knowing that was exactly what he intended to do.

"What else can I do? I'm not going to let someone else get murdered just because I'm a coward."

"But you're the one who's likely to get killed if you do show up." Janna rose and stood over Nolan. "You can't leave. You have to at least notify Scott. He's an undercover cop, in case you weren't aware of it. And let him take care of things outside while you stay here, and—"

"I have to protect that other life. And somehow survive. Not sure how, but I'll figure it out. After all, I do have a good imagination." He stood as well and faced her, smiling grimly. He took her into his arms. "I'm damn worried, Janna. But I have to do something. I'm sure you realize that."

His lips were on hers now, and she felt tears fill her eyes even as they kissed slowly. Sweetly.

She pulled back slightly. "I do understand. But there has to be a way—" And then she thought of something. "I need to send a text. Fast."

"To?" he asked.

"Nella."

He nearly let her go. Would have, if she hadn't continued to hug him with one arm as she reached into her pocket for her cell phone.

"You're asking her to let you out? But don't you have to stop by the clinic to get Wizzy first?"

"Yes, that's right, and I'll probably leave soon," she said. "But I have something else in mind first."

Nolan should have known that the wonderful woman

who'd turned up at his apartment, who'd shown maybe as much concern as he felt after reading that email, wasn't just going to flee.

Janna stayed at his apartment until Scott and Nella arrived. Both wore their standard shelter outfits, just slightly more formal than the T-shirts worn by staffers: denim shirts with a red and brown Chance Animal Shelter logo on the chest pockets, with—what else?—the outline of a dog, although a cat would have worked too.

They knocked softly on the door, and Josh let them in, even though they undoubtedly had a key. And yes, with them, he had to be Josh.

He wasn't sure what Janna had put in her text to Nella, but it definitely hadn't been that she was ready to leave and needed to get the exit gate open.

"So what's going on?" Scott asked as they all stood in the apartment living room. "Janna, your text to Nella said something was terribly wrong and you needed us to meet with you and Josh here." His blue eyes narrowed as he stared first at Janna and then at Josh.

Nella looked less irritated and more concerned. "Should we go sit down and talk?" Her long brown hair flipped sideways with the tilt of her head, her brown eyes worried.

"Sounds good to me," Janna said, and she headed toward the kitchen table and its four chairs. The others followed.

"Where's Wizzy?" Nella asked as they sat down. "Is he okay?"

"Yes. I left him in the clinic for what I thought would be a short while since…since I had a question for Josh about his sticker mailings. I came here to talk because I hadn't seen him a lot today. I'll go get Wizzy when we're through here and head home. But when I first saw Josh, I knew something was wrong. I had to push him a bit to learn what it is. And…it's horrible."

Was this a good idea? Having Scott and Nella here also to learn about that damn email and what had been forwarded to him? He needed to leave the shelter, after all. Maybe their presence would turn out to be a good thing, since they'd surely understand and help him leave—right?

And maybe, just maybe, they'd have some ideas about how he should handle it. Scott was an undercover cop but here in Chance, not San Diego, where Josh needed to go. And Nella was a former cop. But they might have suggestions, or even contacts. And Scott had indicated he was willing to help Nolan.

"So tell us about it," Scott said, looking at Josh.

"Let me show you the email I received." His laptop was still near him on the table. He opened it and brought up the email. He grimaced as he looked at it again. Then he pushed his computer over so both Scott and Nella could see it too.

"Damn," Scott said.

"I can see why you wanted help," Nella added.

He thought about saying it was Janna who wanted help, not him. But heck, if Scott and Nella could provide any ideas, any help, he could definitely use it.

Maybe even to remain alive.

He glanced toward Janna as she sat off to his side,

partly to see her expression—and partly to send her a grateful look of his own.

At least maybe, this way, with at least one undercover cop aware of the email and possibly able to make suggestions, he might survive this after all.

Maybe.

He looked back at Scott. "I have to admit I'm not sure what to do," he said. "You've all been so kind to me here, but right now I think it's time for me to return to my San Diego neighborhood, maybe talk to the authorities there again and see if they'll help keep an eye on the restaurant and its remaining owner. And if I'm there, maybe that owner will be safe."

"But—" Janna began.

Scott interrupted, "You're not just leaving here and doing what that nutcase demands. Don't even think about it. But I have some ideas about what to do."

Really? Nolan could certainly hope Scott would be able to help, but he couldn't count on it. And he definitely wasn't about to allow someone else to be murdered simply because he was protecting himself.

"What should I do, then?" he asked. He could always listen and then decide whether to follow what Scott said.

"Definitely hang out here," Scott insisted. "You know I work with the Chance PD—I'm undercover here, but I'm in close touch with them and still handle some assignments. Nella helps too."

Scott looked at her and she nodded, her expression solemn.

"It's rather late in the day now," Scott continued, "but though I haven't before about your situation, I'll get in touch with those in charge at the police department tonight, and we'll work out a meeting with them tomorrow. We'll figure out a cover story about why you're leaving the shelter for a while, but you'll most likely return while the ultimate plan, whatever it might be, is determined. Okay?"

His stare suggested that it had better be okay.

Maybe the police in Chance had contacts in San Diego, or maybe they could somehow help work things out to protect the other restaurant owner.

Cooperating with Scott, at least as much as he could, might also keep Josh's relationship with the shelter as healthy as possible.

"That's fine with me," Josh said. "I'll certainly cooperate to keep the restaurant owner and myself as safe as possible. I'd like to meet with the authorities, tell them the little I know and let them know I'm ready to do what's necessary. That includes show up in the manner the stalker asks me to, especially if I'll have backup."

He saw a motion out of the corner of his eye and turned slightly. Janna had her lips pursed, and her expression seemed angry. But what did she really want him to do? She didn't know him very well, no matter what he'd actually like to have happen between them.

He wasn't a brave hero type like the protagonists in his story—or in hers. But he wouldn't be able to live with himself if he became the reason for another person's murder. And Janna would just have to deal with that.

Although he liked the idea of her caring enough to want to keep him safe.

"Okay, then," Nella said. "Scott and I will see if

we can work out a meeting with the higher-ups in the CPD tomorrow, with both of us and you there, Josh. Or Nolan."

He laughed. "Whoever I happen to be there—but yes, Nolan sounds right."

"I want to be there too," Janna said, surprising him but only a little. Though he didn't really know her that well—not yet, at least—he was aware she liked to be involved with issues, but this wasn't the same thing as caring for a sick or injured animal.

After all, he wasn't sick or injured…yet.

But she continued, "I'm not sure how much help I can be, if at all. But I do have some friends in San Diego. Maybe I could take some time off and visit with them. I could hang out at the restaurant to observe what's going on. A random passerby shouldn't spark any action from whoever is sending the threats."

"Well," Scott said, "if we work out a time you're not busy at either of your clinics tomorrow, I'm fine with you coming to the CPD meeting and making that kind of suggestion. But—"

"Great," she said. Smiling, she aimed her gaze first at the directors here, then at Nolan.

He wanted to tell her to mind her own business—for her own safety. He also wanted to hug her. Kiss her.

But he just sat there and said, "Thanks, Janna. But as much as I appreciate what you said, I hope the authorities act wisely and tell you to stay here and safe."

"I wish the same for you," she said. "But we'll just have to see how things go and how I can help."

"Like Nolan, you'll have to do what those in charge will tell you," Nella said.

"Absolutely," added Scott. "For now, we'll see you out of the shelter, Janna. But we'll let both of you know when the Chance PD can meet with us all, hopefully tomorrow."

Chapter 17

Back at her condo that night, Janna grabbed a small glass of wine, needing something to fuzz up her mind a bit.

"I'm okay, boy," she said when Wizzy sidled up to her. She gave him a treat.

Nella had accompanied Janna back to the shelter clinic before seeing her out that night, and she'd retrieved her pup, then driven home. Janna wished she had been able to stay with Nolan at his shelter apartment that night, though, as bad an idea as that might be. She knew she wouldn't be able to convince him to remain there and stay safe after talking to the police, rather than going to the restaurant.

She'd seen him shake his head at her as she left with Scott and Nella. He would do his best to make sure she didn't show up at that restaurant, with friends or not.

Well, as she'd mentioned, she actually had some friends in the San Diego area whom she hadn't seen in ages. This might be a good reason to get together with them—not that she'd tell them why. And she certainly wasn't a cop or anyone who could fight off some kind of murderous menace. But she was definitely observant, so maybe she'd be able to provide a small amount of help.

Plus, she'd bring Wizzy along, as usual. He wasn't any kind of K-9 or trained to protect, but he'd jump or bark if anything seemed amiss.

It was almost bedtime now. She'd already sent an email to Kyle to let him know she needed some time off tomorrow, though she didn't know when exactly yet. All she said was that it was another family-related issue.

But she would attend that meeting with the Chance PD, whether it interfered with her time at the downtown clinic or the shelter clinic. Hopefully Kyle would be understanding, without details. There were several other vet techs at the downtown clinic, after all, and nothing major seemed to be going on at the moment at the shelter.

But if Kyle thought someone was needed at either one, he could always get one of the other techs to spell her till she could return. Maybe someone could even take her entire shift tomorrow. She'd be back the following day to take on all her responsibilities—unless she was traveling to San Diego, but she figured that was most likely Friday. But it could be before then to get prepared.

"Let's go out," she told Wizzy, and they took a quick walk outside the condo so he could accomplish what he needed.

When they returned inside, she checked her phone. Sure enough, Kyle had responded. Nice boss that he was, he told her just to keep him informed and he'd work things out.

And so, she was actually able to sleep some that night, although she kept drafting an unsendable email to Nolan in her mind. How was he going to handle things to make sure no one else was hurt? Would *he* be hurt? How would things go for the rest of the week?

Maybe she should be pushier about getting his email address.

Janna hadn't heard about any meetings before it was time to go to the downtown clinic. She started her morning by giving vaccines to several dogs and cats and helping Kyle examine a new litter of puppies. That was fun.

But she hadn't been able to check her phone for nearly an hour.

Fortunately, when she left the exam for the puppies, she saw a text from Scott saying the meeting would be at two that afternoon at the Chance Police Department downtown.

It wasn't quite noon yet, so that worked well. Her shift at the shelter clinic was scheduled to start at one, so she hurried to Kyle's office.

He was handling paperwork from the puppy exam, and she was able to tell him more specifically about her time conflict that afternoon.

"That's fine," he told her, fortunately. He would bring Betty, another vet tech, to the shelter when he headed there later, he told her. Janna liked Betty a lot, so she was happy with that—although she hoped she didn't like working at the shelter so much that she'd try to take Janna's place there in the future.

She asked if it was okay to leave Wizzy at the downtown clinic for now. Taking her dog to the police station didn't sound like a good idea. Kyle was fine with it, as long as Wizzy stayed in one of the usual dog enclosures in the back. He'd stayed there before, and although Janna recognized it wasn't his favorite way to spend time, she knew he'd be fine there.

"I'll pick you up later," she told Wizzy.

The police station was in the town's civic center, not far from the clinic, so Janna was able to walk there. And wasn't surprised to see Scott, Nella and Nolan standing at the reception desk and talking to the officer behind it.

None of them wore Chance Animal Shelter shirts— just plain T-shirts with jackets. Janna, of course, was also in a neutral outfit, without her scrubs.

She joined them quickly. "Hi," she said. "When does our meeting start?" She used the word *our* on purpose. They knew she intended to join them. She was part of this.

"Pretty soon," Nella told her. "We're going to be shown to an office upstairs."

And in fact, another officer came up to them as soon as Scott walked away from the desk. "Please follow me," she said, and led them to an elevator.

They headed for the third floor, which appeared to be the top one in the building. Janna attempted to stay near Nolan, but he was mostly talking with Scott so she wound up closer to Nella. No time to talk about how things were at the shelter—although Janna figured all was okay at the moment. And after all, what was going on with Nolan shouldn't affect the shelter. Right?

They were shown into an office with a sign outside indicating it belonged to Police Chief Andrew Shermovski.

"Come in," said their escorting officer. Only then did

Janna notice that the shield on her uniform pocket said Assistant Chief Kara Province. The tall, slender officer with short, wavy black hair was most likely one of the authorities they'd be meeting with.

The office was large, with a substantial metal desk facing the door. Another man in uniform stood up from behind it. The police chief, Janna surmised.

Sure enough, Scott soon introduced her and Nolan to Chief Andrew Shermovski and Assistant Chief Province.

Chief Shermovski appeared to be in his sixties. His dark eyes, framed with wrinkles, appeared interested yet wary. He was tall and slim, with short salt-and-pepper hair. "Welcome," he said. "Please sit down, all of you." He gestured at the many low-back chairs facing his desk, and Janna joined the others, crossing the laminated wooden floor and taking one of the seats.

Hers, fortunately, was beside Nolan's, though she was on the end. She felt she was there to support him—sort of. But not any haywire idea of his about showing up at the restaurant in San Diego just because his stalker told him to, so he could potentially be killed instead of the restaurant owner.

Scott sat on Nolan's other side, and Nella sat beside Scott.

"I'm Chief Shermovski of the Chance PD," the man said. "But you can call me Sherm. And you can call Assistant Police Chief Kara Province—" he gestured to the woman who was moving a chair next to him "—Assistant Police Chief Kara Province."

She laughed as she sat down. "Kara will do," she said.

"So," Sherm said, looking at Nolan, "Scott has filled

it as to what's going on, including who you are
ou're currently a staff member at the Chance
elter. I know the place well. But he also told
ecently received some communication sug-
need to show up someplace else, and that
tion might have been sent by the person
brought you to the shelter in the first place.
need some help from police in a differ-
with it. How about telling me more?"
d Nolan's face as the chief spoke. It re-
ne, but it seemed to have gone stony.
hat might be how the poor guy was deal-
mpossible situation.
uld only hope that it would wind up being less
ble with the help of the police in this room.

n stared at Chief Sherm as he told him his
he was a successful novelist but he and his agent
blicist had started receiving threats by email and
. They had started after publication of his latest
selling novel, which was loosely based on a true
ne that had occurred last year—the murder of Jaxon
ybell, one of the two owners of the Great Meals Res-
rant in San Diego.

He'd fictionalized it in his book, of course. It had a
suitable ending, a killer caught with evidence against
him sufficient for conviction. That killer wasn't actually based on any real suspect that he'd heard of. The
idea was to get more publicity into the actual case, so
the local police would dig even further and figure it out.

Which hadn't happened.

The threats against Nolan began soon afte[r]
cation, he explained. Things had happened,
fire and gunshot at his home. He was in trou[ble]
wanted to live. And in his research for this b[ook he]
heard of the Chance Animal Shelter and rur[al]
it was really about. He was grateful to be
cently as a staff member.

He finally aimed a glance at Janna. H[e]
seemed horrified, even though she'd hea[rd]
But she was staring at him, her brows fu[rrowed]
as if she hurt on his behalf.

"The thing is, my agent just received
I'm sure Scott's told you about—threateni[ng]
ing owner of the Great Meals Restaurant if I d[on't show]
up there on Friday. I'm planning on going, but
any contacts in San Diego who can help watch
maybe arrest the stalker before they can do anyt[hing."]

"Let's talk about that," Sherm agreed. The
chief had seemed quite familiar with pretty mu[ch ev]
erything Nolan had said, no doubt thanks to Sco[tt get]
ting in touch with him earlier.

"I appreciate that," Nolan said.

"Before you got here, I talked this over with Ka[thy,"]
Sherm went on. "We considered coming to the shelte[r to]
talk to you but figured it'd be too easy for some of yo[ur]
staff members to spot us there and start asking ques[-]
tions. Sneaking you here seemed better." He looked at
Scott, who nodded.

"This worked out fine." Scott sounded certain enough
that Nolan assumed he was right. At least he hoped he was.

"Also," Sherm continued, "we considered getting in

touch with some of our contacts at the San Diego Police Department and sending you down there. But—well, we decided that was a bad idea, although we will communicate with those contacts. But what would be a good idea is if that person comes here to Chance to get you—and we can apprehend him then."

Interesting, Nolan thought. "So exactly how is that going to happen?"

"And how are we going to protect the shelter if that person comes to Chance?" Scott added.

"We won't tell them about the shelter," Sherm promised, "but we'll be prepared. Here's what we have in mind. Who was it who received that new threat? Your agent, you said?"

"That's right." Nolan hadn't yet mentioned Bruce's name, but he would if it made sense later.

"Well, here's what I want you to do," Sherm said. "I assume you can get back in touch with your agent, maybe call him or her from here."

"If I get access to a phone," Nolan said, glancing at Scott, "I'd be glad to call him."

"We'll work that out while you're here." Sherm nodded. "We'll want to tell your agent to contact the person who's been anonymously in touch with him by sending a response email—and we'll want that email address, by the way."

"I'll ask him for it," Nolan agreed.

"Good. We'll want your agent's name and contact information, too, but you can do the follow-up for now."

"It's Bruce Ashcourt, and I can get you his information."

"Fine. So, when Bruce sends that email, he should let that person know you're currently in Chance." He looked at Scott again. "Not mentioning the shelter but that you're researching a new story and hanging out briefly in town and popping in at the nearby Chance K-9 Ranch for that research."

Nolan was aware that there was a K-9 ranch located in the hills near Chance, where they brought in and trained potential military and therapy dogs. It actually might make an interesting background for a story or two, but he hadn't started researching anything like that.

"So the person would then think I'm in this area for a different reason." Nolan liked that idea—as long as that jerk of a person was captured without learning about the Chance Animal Shelter.

"Exactly. We'll hope that the killer shows up in this area, though not anywhere near the shelter—which is pretty secure anyway—hunting you as their prey. Our whole Chance PD will be aware of it, of course, and be prepared to take that person into custody."

"Sounds good to me," Nolan said. He was glad when Kara also seemed onboard. She appeared to be the most involved. And Scott and Nella, undoubtedly worried about the shelter, also seemed onboard.

And Janna? "It does sound better than having you travel to San Diego and trust cops there that you haven't met to keep you safe," she said. Good. She was okay with it as well, not that she could control what he did.

But somehow, he wanted to make her happy with it.

"Excellent," Sherm said. "As I said, I'll also contact the San Diego PD to notify them what's going on and ask again who their most likely suspects are so we can keep our eyes out for them. Meanwhile, Kara can take you into one of our waiting rooms and bring in a burner phone so you can call your agent. Do you know his phone number?"

They'd been connected long enough that Nolan had memorized Bruce's phone number. He easily forwarded the information to potential publishers and anyone else he wanted to connect with Bruce.

Then Sherm said that Nolan's agent should also ask for the stalker's phone number so Nolan could call them. For that, Nolan could keep the burner phone.

That sounded as if it had potential. Would he actually get to speak with the jerk who'd been threatening him? If so, could he keep his cool?

He'd have to, to lure them here to Chance to talk with him. Oh, and if that person just happened to be taken into custody by local authorities here… That definitely sounded good.

Right now, he was just as glad when Scott and Nella said they would hang out with Sherm and Kara while he talked to Bruce, unless there was something he wanted them to hear.

"I'll tell you," Nolan promised, "if anything comes up in the conversation that you should know about. And I will tell Bruce to give me the person's email address, in case you can track them down that way."

"Unlikely, but thanks," Sherm said.

Too bad Bruce was unlikely to get that person's phone number right away too. But hopefully that would come later.

In a few minutes, Kara led Nolan and Janna down a short hallway outside Sherm's office. No one was there to look at them, though it was unlikely he'd be recognized. Janna might be known as a local vet tech, but her real reason to be around at that time wouldn't be obvious.

Soon, Kara left them in another, smaller office, with a desk that had notepaper and pens on top. She stayed only for a few minutes at first. She returned shortly with a brand-name cell phone and handed it to Nolan. "This is one of the phones we keep here. We get its number changed often, and we keep its GPS off. No one should be able to track you down if you use it, so you could go ahead and call your agent."

"Thanks," Nolan said, then watched Kara leave. Janna remained with him. "This should be interesting." He checked his watch for the time. Just past three o'clock. Bruce would still be working. But would he answer a phone call from a strange number?

Fortunately, he did. "Bruce Ashcourt," he said. "Who's calling?"

"Bruce, this is Nolan."

"What! Where are you? This isn't your regular phone number. Are you okay? What's going on?"

Nolan considered Bruce a friend as well as a professional colleague, and it felt somewhat good to hear him ask questions as if he gave a damn about him too.

"I'm fine," Nolan said, glancing at Janna in the chair beside him. "But—I'm trying to deal with that…situation."

"You mean the damn email threatening the restaurant owner? Don't tell me you're actually going to show up in San Diego."

Nolan looked Janna in the eyes. She was glaring as if she half expected him to say he would do exactly that to save a life. But he'd received his instructions from Chief Sherm, and they sounded reasonable to him.

"No, but I do want to make sure the restaurant owner isn't hurt, if I can. And I'd like your help."

"Sure," Bruce said. "What can I do?"

"Well, first I'd like you to give me the email address the threatening communication came from." He heard a slight protest, but before Bruce could interrupt, Nolan continued, "I realize we can't be sure it's real or that they'll check it again, but just in case…"

"Okay. I printed it out and kept the copy in my desk, here. Just a minute… Here it is."

Bruce read it off. It was a generic Gmail address. Well, it didn't hurt to have it—and pass it along to his police contacts, just in case it helped them.

"Thanks," Nolan told Bruce. "And here's how I'd like you to help me. I know it sounds strange, but I'm hoping it helps the authorities find and arrest that menace."

Nolan explained that he wanted Bruce to respond to that email address and tell the person he had information about Nolan to convey. "You can provide this phone number too, if you want. Hopefully, the person will look at your email and respond, one way or the other."

Nolan asked Bruce to say that Nolan wasn't coming to the restaurant but was willing to talk to whoever it was, not in San Diego, but in Chance, California, if they can just have a brief meeting—Nolan also promised not to write about it.

"You can let them know that I said I assume my book might have been too close to reality, too close to outing the actual perpetrator, but after I meet with the person, I'll make it clearer online and in my other appearances that my stories may be based on true events but they're fiction. Whoever appears to be the killer in the actual homicide isn't the real one."

"I'm not sure that's what that jerk is driving at," Bruce said, "but they might actually want to talk to you in person. But—damn, Nolan, you might really be put in danger that way."

Nolan couldn't help glancing at Janna, beside him. She appeared ashen and horrified, but she pressed her lips together and nodded. "Bruce, this is Janna," she introduced herself, "a new friend of Nolan's. I'm aware of what he's up to, and you should know that he's got some official contacts who will help him if he meets with that person. They'll protect him, and hopefully nab that person."

Nolan had been about to say the same thing, but he appreciated Janna getting involved.

"I was hoping that was the situation," Bruce said. "Okay. I'll do it, but you can be sure I'm not thrilled about it. Or at least I'll do it if you promise to be damned careful, Nolan."

Still looking into Janna's eyes, Nolan nodded—not that Bruce could see him. "I promise."

Chapter 18

The meeting with the police was over. So was Nolan's talk with his agent. Janna had eavesdropped—and participated.

She was on her own again now as Scott and Nella saw Nolan back to the shelter. On her own in downtown Chance, where it was just early evening, and people were walking around the civic center. Janna felt safe enough on her own, as she did all the time here, even later at night.

This was Chance, after all.

But as she walked the few streets between the police station and the downtown veterinary clinic, she couldn't help wondering what things would be like on Friday. Assuming Nolan's agent Bruce actually got in contact with the person who'd emailed him, and then passed along what Nolan had asked him to.

Would that person get in contact with Nolan to set up a time and place to meet here in Chance? She gathered that Nolan would still have the phone he'd received that day, and his agent should have the phone number to pass along.

Most likely they'd speak by phone, though she knew

Nolan would only be able to turn it on at times and locations that were approved by Scott—maybe at the shelter but only for short periods of time so he couldn't be
found. But how would Nolan be able to set up a meeting where the cops would also be around, and not seen
by the guy they needed to nab?

Okay, she was overthinking this. She was a veterinary technician, not in any aspect of law enforcement.

But she was certainly permitted to worry about the
guy she'd respected before as a best-selling author, who'd
now also become a friend and lover.

She hoped there could be even more between them
than a single night together.

But he had to survive in any case.

She'd reached the Chance Veterinary Clinic. It was
still early enough that she figured the door into the waiting room would be open.

She was right. She peeked into Kyle's office. Seated
at his desk, he looked up at her.

"Sorry I didn't get back earlier, but I should be available all day tomorrow," she said.

"Everything okay with your family?" he asked, and
the nice veterinarian who was her boss looked concerned.

And heck, she'd already been thinking about her
dream that Nolan could become more than a friend.
Family? Not likely, but family issues was the excuse
she'd given Kyle for her unavailability earlier.

"Pretty much," she said. "Some things still need to be
worked out." She said that in case she wound up needing some more time off—like, on Friday. "But it's all
improving."

Fortunately, Kyle didn't ask for more details.

"Anything you need for me to do this evening?" she asked. She wanted to still be a team player here, even though her mind was swirling with all the things going on around her—among them Nolan.

Kyle asked her to go check on a few of the animals staying overnight to make sure they were doing okay: a dog she'd worked with before, a couple of newcomers, and four cats in the clinic enclosures.

Most of the dogs appeared calm, even lethargic, and when she checked the records near their enclosures, she confirmed they remained under some degree of sedation.

One dog she worked with seemed more energetic, though, and Janna knew that English bulldog mix Rennie was nearly ready to go home to her family, probably tomorrow.

The cats all seemed interested to see her. Maybe they were nearly ready to be released as well.

Soon, it was time to pop in and tell Kyle the results of her visits, which she'd noted on the records. Then it was time to go get Wizzy and head home.

But after eating dinner and taking Wizzy outside again for a short while, she spent some time editing her manuscript on her laptop.

Janna often wrote and edited after work, but these days she couldn't help wondering what Nolan might think of her changes.

She spent quite a while with it that night, which again wasn't unusual. Eventually, though, she got too tired to concentrate, so she took Wizzy outside again. Back in her bedroom, she read part of a book she'd started—not

Nolan's. She'd already finished his most recent one, of course. She'd had a hard time putting it down to get some sleep or go to work.

At bedtime, she played with Wizzy a bit. She adored her wonderful dog. But it still would be nice to have more human company at night.

She wondered how Nolan was doing. Could he already have heard back from his stalker? Had his agent been able to contact them, and had they responded already?

After watching a little TV in bed, she managed to fall asleep—after, yes, thinking again about Nolan and how he was doing that night.

But on Tuesday morning, she had her shift downtown first thing. She got there early and placed Wizzy in his enclosure after a nice long walk at home and feeding him well, as usual. Kyle hadn't yet arrived, but Janna interacted with a couple of the other vet staff, glad to see them and be in her usual surroundings here.

Still, she looked forward to heading to the shelter.

Would she get to see Nolan that day? If so, only from a distance? Or would she be able to get him alone and talk about what was happening?

Early that afternoon, her shift at the downtown clinic ended after a relatively calm day. She wrapped things up with Kyle as usual, and he told her he wouldn't be joining her at the shelter clinic that day unless something was wrong there. That wasn't unusual, and she told him she would call him if necessary, though she hoped she didn't need to.

At the shelter clinic at last, Janna got Nella to let her in.

"Everything okay?" Janna asked the assistant director. After all, Nella knew what was going on. "Has... has you-know-who heard from that person?" No need to be more specific, she figured.

"Don't know. But he's out doing some training. Maybe you can check with him before heading to the clinic. I've already looked in on the animals a couple of times, and everything there seems fine." Nella paused. "You and he seem to be getting somewhat close."

Oh dear. It was bad enough Janna was more interested in Nolan than made sense, but others were seeing it as well. She decided to hopefully aim Nella's thoughts in another, though still relevant, direction.

"Sorry it seems so obvious," Janna said quietly. "I've been trying my hand at writing a book, and as you're aware, I know who Josh really is. He's read some of my manuscript and has been giving me advice."

There. That should explain why they might have spent more time together than they otherwise should—except for Janna's helping him mail his signature stickers.

"Got it. Well, I can understand even more why you give a damn about him. And—good luck with that, though we need your vet tech skills around here." Then Nella headed toward the offices before Janna could assure her she had no intention of giving up her real career.

At least not anytime soon.

But she could always hope her writing would eventually get somewhere, with or without Nolan's help.

Janna left her laptop in the clinic, then took Wizzy

out to the shelter's central path. Just for a short while,
she told herself. After all, as the vet tech around here,
she needed to check on the animals under the shelter's
care. She was glad, though, that Nella stopped in and
provided her input on the situation and the well-being
of the animals. And it didn't hurt to give Wizzy another
walk before kenneling him again.

Outside, she wasn't surprised to see the usual: a lot
of staff members working with dogs and each other.
She headed toward them with her own pup, greeting
people as she reached them, including Bibi and Augie
and Chessie with some shelter dogs who'd been around
for a while.

Janna was already pondering what she'd do if she
saw Josh. *When* she saw Josh. She'd hang around at the
shelter till she did. She wanted to find out if he'd heard
anything more about Friday and what was to occur in
downtown Chance.

One way or another, would that be the last time she'd
be seeing him? After all, with luck, they'd bring in the
person whose terrible threats had brought Nolan to the
shelter.

With bad luck—

No, she didn't want to even think about what might
happen to Nolan if things went wrong.

But that *when* didn't happen now. Without even
glimpsing Josh while she was out there, it was time to
return to the clinic.

First, she took Wizzy to one of the larger rooms since
he'd be there on his own for a while. She gave him a bowl
of water and some of his usual chew toys to keep him

occupied. Then, it was time to look in on her charges for the day.

Bambam, Baxter and Minnie were still in their respective enclosures. Not Mika, though. Janna would check that sweet beagle mix's chart to be sure, but she figured Kyle had released her back to her regular kennel. She wanted to cheer. Better yet, hug Mika. She'd try looking in on her later.

Not much to do now, fortunately. That was often the case as long as none of their patients was doing poorly, and there were no new arrivals.

Too bad she couldn't just go find Josh and bring him in to give her advice. After all, that was one reason she brought her laptop. But she hoped to work a bit on her story if she had time between checking on the animals here and visiting those outside.

It wasn't her usual routine at the shelter, but it would keep her mind occupied instead of worrying so much about Friday.

In fact—she had an idea. One that had been percolating in her mind.

Bring Josh to the clinic? Too obvious. And it might look odd if she headed to his apartment with him. But the apartment for the clinic personnel was sort of off by itself in the apartment building. Its key was in the desk here. She wouldn't stay there tonight. But maybe she could get just a little alone time with Josh there this afternoon.

The reason she'd give him was to go over her latest thoughts about her manuscript. But what she really wanted was some kind of assurance from him that he'd be fine, even after Friday.

After retrieving the key and checking on the patients and Wizzy once more, Janna left the clinic with her laptop. As surreptitiously as possible, she headed to the apartment building. Fortunately, she didn't see anyone and didn't believe anyone saw her.

The vet staff apartment looked fine, pretty much like Josh's and probably everyone else's did at the shelter. But Janna checked it thoroughly and didn't see any indications of anyone else staying there recently except for her.

She left her laptop in the apartment, then headed down to the central walking area again. How could she best search for Josh?

Fortunately, she didn't have to come up with a plan. He was out now, walking Spike, surrounded by other staffers and dogs.

Janna headed into the crowd, patting some of the pups on the head and saying hi to the staff members. She circled to avoid getting close to Josh initially, but eventually she was able to pat Spike on the head and say hi.

Unlike with the others, she drew closer to Josh. "I've got some questions for you, mostly about my—you know what." She figured he'd assume it was her writing. But she had other questions for him too, about his own safety. And right now, that was even more important.

He looked at her quizzically but nodded, as if asking when and where they could talk.

"I may stay overnight tonight, so I'm checking out the apartment for the clinic staff." Her gaze was a silent invitation for him to join her.

"About ten minutes?" he whispered.

She nodded, then walked away. And hoped they'd actually be able to meet up there and then.

For the next few minutes, she popped into the shelter buildings. First was the one for cats and small animals. All appeared fine as she peered through the wire mesh of the enclosures. Next came the large dogs, then the medium dogs—Mika was indeed back in her usual enclosure—and finally the small dog building. Not that she could really tell much, walking through them so quickly, but she didn't see any animals in distress. Fortunately, both Mika and Squeegee had seemed fine.

She said hi to a lot of staff members, and back outside, she briefly patted a few of the dogs they were walking. Then she headed toward the clinic.

Only she kept going, making her way to the apartment building, glad she ran into no staffers there. She hurried to the apartment for clinic personnel.

She had left the door unlocked earlier, just in case. Not usually a good idea, but if Nolan got there first, he could just pop inside.

Which he had. He was sitting in the living room area on one of the chairs.

Janna quickly closed and locked the door behind her. "Hi," she said.

"Hi back." He came toward her. "Everything okay?"

"With me? Sure, except that I'm worried about you."

"I'm fine. And I intend to stay that way." They were face-to-face now.

Janna wasn't sure which of them reached out first.

Maybe it was simultaneous. But suddenly they were in each other's arms, kissing hotly.

Unwise? Sure. But it had been so long since they'd even gotten to talk, let alone touch. And it felt so wonderful to have his lips on hers, his tongue in her mouth, his hands feeling up and down the back of her body...

Okay. She couldn't resist. "The bedroom is this way," she gasped against him—as if this apartment wasn't exactly like his.

Soon, they were lying together, naked, on top of the comforter.

Their lovemaking was even hotter, yet somehow more tender, than the wonderful experience she'd had before with this man.

When they lay in each other's arms, both breathing hard, both still placing their hands and lips on the other, Janna couldn't help saying, "Please, Nolan. Even if this is our last time together—I couldn't bear it if anything happened to you. Please don't try to meet with the person who's been threatening you. Who knows if the police—"

"I understand your concern, my love," he whispered against her mouth. "But to make sure I survive, and stop the threats, I need to at least try to help bring them in."

And then he started stroking her again.

The sex had been incredible. Again.

And he had called Janna *my love*.

Nolan hadn't thought about it in advance. It just came out.

But he had really fallen for this lovely, sexy writer who

loved animals enough to save their lives. Plus, he adored her concern for him.

But he had to do what he had to do, to save not only his own life but also Declan, the remaining restaurant owner.

So far, there'd been no response to the request that the person show up in Chance, assuming Bruce had actually sent it. And Nolan trusted his agent, so he felt fairly sure—

"Nolan? What are you thinking?"

He and Janna had left the bed ten minutes ago, dressing quickly. Nolan knew he needed to sneak back to the main shelter area again without being seen. But at the moment, he was holding Janna in his arms again.

"I'm thinking how great it is to be holding you this way."

"I love holding you too," she said, looking up at him. "But before I asked, you seemed to slow what we were doing a little, so I figured your mind was wandering."

"Yeah, it was," he admitted. "And I'm sorry, love, but I do need to go work things out for Friday, even though you don't like the idea."

"Love," she repeated softly. "I know that's just a sweet way of addressing me, but—well, just in case you're wondering, and in case it means something, I think I'm falling in love with you too. I understand, though, why you feel you have to do something on Friday. But—"

"But I'm hoping it will help me get back to my real life. And maybe develop something more with you. Here, we can't be together much, and we have to hide it when we are. But if that jerk is finally caught before they can act on what they've threatened, I'll be able to leave this lovely shelter for good. And then I can see you without hiding it, and hopefully we can figure out a way to be together more."

"I wish," Janna breathed. "But I'm just so scared that something will go wrong."

"I can't guarantee it won't. But I have to try. And right now, I need to leave and return to my temporary life as Josh, such as it is, here at the shelter." He bent down and kissed her again—long and hard, so hard that his body started reacting yet again. He pulled away. "Besides," he said, "I bet Wizzy misses you."

"And I always miss my pup when we have to be apart," she admitted. "Guess it'll be best if I leave first. I can intercept anyone who happens to be around so they won't see you."

"Sounds good," Nolan said.

But he couldn't help missing Janna too when she left his presence.

Who knew when they'd have time together again like this, if ever?

After waiting for ten minutes, he figured it was time for him to leave too. Fortunately, he didn't see anyone, and so he sneaked around to his apartment on the fourth floor. That way, if someone did happen to notice his presence, he could always say he'd been hanging out there for a while.

He'd need to go to dinner soon, but right now he had a call he wanted to make on that loaner phone. He turned it on and called Bruce again.

"Hi, Nolan," his agent said after answering right

away. "I wasn't sure when a good time to call you was, but I wanted to let you know that I did send the email we discussed to the person who sent that troubling email to me. I let them know you needed to talk to them about how to deal with...well, Friday. I gave them your new phone number too. They got back to me and said they'd call you around nine tonight. I hope that's all right."

"Fine," Nolan said. He'd have plenty of time to eat, then return here to his apartment. He thanked Bruce, then, after they hung up and he turned the phone off, he hurried down to the cafeteria.

No Janna here tonight, unsurprisingly. But he did get to eat with Scott and Nella. Not that he could talk about what was on his mind at all here, even a little. But when Nella asked if everything was okay with him, a nice general question, he said yes.

In fact, he wasn't about to tell her how well everything had gone with him earlier today, but his mind did race to recall Janna's gorgeous face—not that she was ever out of his thoughts for long.

He also wasn't about to mention the call he was anticipating that night till after it had occurred.

Josh peeked in on his buddy Spike in his enclosure after dinner and even took him for a short walk. Others would already have fed him, but Nolan—Josh at the moment—gave Spike a treat from the building's supply.

Back at his apartment, he removed the phone he'd kept hidden in his pocket and turned it on again, then switched on the TV as he waited.

At nine, he stared at the phone. Nothing yet.

Five minutes later, the phone rang. Nolan turned the TV off and answered. "Hello?"

"Nolan Hoffsler, I believe you were anticipating this call. I'm the person who has been in touch with Bruce Ashcourt, trying to communicate with you." The voice was choppy and shrill and definitely disguised, Nolan thought. "Like I said, I want to meet with you on Friday at the Great Meals Restaurant so we can talk about your book. If you don't show up, Declan will die. Will you be there?"

That shrill, demanding voice made Nolan shudder. He wished he could just hang up. Shut off this phone. But he knew better. He didn't want to be the cause of anyone's death.

And so he said what he'd been told to by the Chance authorities. "Sorry, but I can't come to San Diego on Friday."

He heard a gasp of most likely rage, so he continued quickly.

"But yes, I'll meet with you. I'm in the middle of some important research for my next book, at a K-9 ranch. I'll definitely take some time off to talk, but you'll need to come to where I am instead. It's only a few hours' drive from San Diego."

He drew in his breath. Here it was. He was giving away the town where he was located, but not all the details. Still—okay, he knew the police were on board.

"Where the hell are you?" the voice practically screamed.

"Chance, California," Nolan blurted, closing his eyes.

"I'd like to meet you at a restaurant here on Friday. You can choose the time. Will you be here?"

A pause, and then, "Yes, damn it. I'll be there."

Chapter 19

The good thing? After accomplishing her work at the downtown clinic on Wednesday and Thursday, Janna spent more time than usual at the shelter, mostly checking on the animals in the clinic there, who fortunately seemed to be doing okay, and no more were brought in.

That meant she saw more of Josh out with the staff members and could spend time with him as she observed the shelter animals.

Josh still worked almost exclusively with former K-9 Spike despite apparently indicating he'd like to have other canine friends here too, and Janna sometimes worked with Wizzy the way the staff members here did. That meant her pup ran when Spike did, fetched toys and obeyed the usual commands.

When Janna talked with Josh, no one seemed particularly interested in their closeness, although she sometimes found herself trading looks with Nella when the assistant director came out to observe.

But as evening drew closer and staff members headed to dinner, Janna took Wizzy to the clinic, then Josh and she headed separately to the clinic apartment for a while. To talk.

To do more. A lot more. But very quickly.

And Janna wound up also going to the cafeteria for dinner on both of those nights before heading home with Wizzy.

The bad thing? As much as Janna enjoyed those afternoons, both in public somewhat with Josh and the times they were together alone—especially the times when they were alone—her mind never left the anticipation of Friday and what might occur.

The more Janna was with Josh, the more she cared… and the more she knew she would be absolutely devastated if anything happened to him.

And so, after they made love, she often tried to begin a conversation about what was likely to happen. She tried to talk him out of the proposed meeting, to ask the cops to have someone undercover pretend to be him.

To no avail.

She couldn't talk herself out of caring so much about him either. Sure, he was a good writer, and when she wrote a few paragraphs alone at home with Wizzy at night and showed them to Nolan when they got together, he gave her even more critiques that she considered helpful. So he was pretty much a professional advisor.

That was all, she tried to tell herself.

Right.

Maybe she'd have been able to convince herself if they hadn't engaged in such wonderful, though brief, sexual encounters. She'd fortunately stocked up on condoms and hid them in her pockets. Josh obviously wasn't able to go out and obtain any.

Now it was Friday morning. At the moment, she remained in bed, but she'd get up soon.

She didn't really know what the schedule was supposed to be, only that at some point Scott and Nella would accompany Josh downtown to meet up with the stalker. Had all the arrangements been made? Did Josh know where and when they'd be meeting?

If so, he hadn't let her know, which wasn't a good thing.

Wizzy rose when she did. "Good morning, boy," she told him, then bent to give her warm, furry pup a hug, because she could. Because he was there. And because she needed some emotional support.

She showered, dressed, then took Wizzy out for a short walk. At the downtown vet clinic, Janna's help was needed almost immediately during a surgical procedure on a Labrador retriever with an internal blockage. It all worked out well and fairly quickly.

Since Janna went to the shelter clinic daily, another vet tech was put in charge of looking in on the Lab on and off that afternoon.

Janna went into Kyle's office to let him know she was on her way. Fortunately, it was still morning. Surely Nolan wouldn't be downtown yet—right?

"Good job," her boss said, looking up at her with a smile from where he sat at his desk. "I'll see you later at the shelter."

"I'm heading there now," she said. "But if everything—everyone—appears to be doing well, I'd like to leave soon, maybe even before you arrive." She fumbled inside for a reason to give him that would make sense without giving away what she really wanted to do.

"Everything okay?" he asked.

No, she wanted to shout.

But before she responded at all, he continued, "Your family?"

Well, as she'd thought before, she kind of considered Nolan family now. "In a way," she said. "But—"

"Okay, you don't have to talk about it. I'll just give you some extra time off without explanation, maybe in recognition of the good job you did earlier with that Lab's procedure. I know you'll make up for it. You always spend a lot of time at both clinics, and I appreciate it."

And Janna wanted to tell Kyle how much she appreciated his understanding, without actually knowing what she was up to. "Thanks," was all she said. "Maybe I'll see you later. In any case, I'll see you here tomorrow."

Saturday. She rarely took even weekends off, although she'd stay away for an occasional Saturday or Sunday now and then.

She retrieved Wizzy from his enclosure and got them both into the car to go to the shelter.

How would Janna be able to stay near enough to Nolan to make sure he was being well taken care of? She figured Scott and Nella would bring Nolan out of the shelter and take him to wherever the Chance police wanted him. Janna would ask Nella if she could tag along, although she figured she knew what the answer would be.

She doubted that Scott or Nella would be right there

as they waited for the stalker to appear, even though
they were cops. Those in charge might not want the
undercover officers put into danger. Never mind that it
would be okay to do that to Nolan. But he was the key
to this working.

She, however, definitely was not. Neither Nella nor
Scott was likely to want her anywhere around whatever
might happen.

So she wouldn't ask. She'd keep her eyes open and
just happen to leave whenever Josh was escorted from
the shelter. And if she happened to drive wherever they
happened to head—well, just coincidence. Or so she'd
tell them if they wound up noticing and giving her a
hard time.

Could she help to save Nolan? Who knew?

But she'd want to be there, just in case.

Scott asked Josh to come to his office first thing that
Friday morning to receive thanks about how well he had
been working with Spike. Or at least that was the excuse
others might have heard.

Nolan was to tell the stalker to meet him late that afternoon at a popular hangout in town, Scott told him,
the Joint Restaurant. That way, if the person knew the
area or did viable research, they'd think it was a good
place to get together with Nolan—and maybe grab him.

Nolan gathered that the Chance PD had a good relationship with the Joint's owners. They'd get the place
set up, maybe with just a few patrons who were undercover. Hopefully they'd not only nab the perpetrator but
would also keep Nolan safe.

"We'll leave here around three o'clock," Scott said from behind his desk in the shelter office. "We'll need for you to dress in regular clothes." Not his current Chance Animal Shelter T-shirt, but Nolan had already figured that out.

"Right now, though, how about getting in touch with that person while we're here?"

"Okay if I text them?" Nolan asked.

But even though Nolan had described the screechy voice as difficult to listen to, Scott and Nella wanted him to make personal contact—though they promised not to interrupt.

At least the stalker had confirmed they were available at the number they'd called Nolan from before. He'd given that number to Scott, who gave it to Sherm, but in the end trying to find the person with the number was useless. It had been a burner phone like the one Nolan had been given. They hadn't been able to determine its location.

"All right. I'll call them now." Nolan turned his phone on.

The call was answered right away. "Hoffsler?" the voice said. "We're still meeting this afternoon, right?"

Oh yes, it was the same shrill, loud, disguised voice. Nolan glanced from Scott to Nella and saw them grimacing.

"I've made a reservation at one of Chance's main restaurants," Nolan confirmed. "The Joint, at three thirty. Will you be there?"

"Don't try anything stupid. We'll talk. I want to know more about your stupid story and your research and what it had to do with what really happened at that damn Great Meals Restaurant in San Diego."

That was the only reason that person wanted to meet? Hah!

"And the remaining owner of Great Meals won't be hurt if we meet in Chance, right?" Nolan had to ask.

"He'll be fine."

But I won't, most likely, Nolan thought, *if this person has anything to do with it.*

"Great," he said nevertheless. "See you at three thirty at the Joint."

Was the person still on the phone? Probably not. There was no response.

Nolan ended the call and turned the phone off, then looked at Scott. "I assume you'll let Sherm know," he said.

"Yes, and the Joint's owners. They're already aware they'll need to shoo all patrons out of there this afternoon. We'll have some of our own folks show up and start eating there before our scheduled time."

"Got it," Nolan said. "And I assume I'm just to act like normal around here till just a while before three."

"That's right."

And so Nolan left the office, his phone of the moment stuffed way down into his pocket with some tissues so there'd be an apparent reason for that pocket to appear occupied. He could always blow his nose if anyone asked about it.

He spent his time in the yard with Spike, being Josh again, working with his best canine buddy around there as well as some of his staffer friends.

Would he see any of them again after this afternoon?

Even more important, he had an urge to pop into the shelter's vet clinic. It should be around the time Janna would arrive. Maybe—

Hey, had she heard his thoughts? Janna was just coming out the door of the clinic, Wizzy leashed beside her.

Josh and Spike headed in their direction.

For a while, he worked with Spike while Janna worked with Wizzy, doing the usual commands and running around the yard, with other staff members joining them with the dogs they were training.

Josh was even panting a bit when they slowed down. Oh yes, working with the dogs was fun—and with Janna's presence, it was even better.

But time was passing. Could they break away even for a short time before he had to get ready for that afternoon?

In fact… He approached Janna and said loudly, "I knew you already had Wizzy trained well, but he seems to be getting even better." Much more softly, he added, "I have to go change clothes after lunch. Can you come to my apartment?"

This time her voice was loud as she responded, "I love watching all of you train dogs here and think Wizzy has a lot of fun when I work with him here too. And I'm also able to keep an eye on the other pups to make sure none seems to have any health issues." Then, softly, she said, "I'll have lunch here too, then head there."

As she walked away with Wizzy, Josh looked around. A few other staff members were near them, but not too close. None should have been able to hear anything about going to his apartment.

But lunch? He wasn't hungry, but he did need to return Spike to his enclosure. At the cafeteria, he got just a little food from the counter, then sat down with some other staff members—not Scott or Nella.

Janna soon came in with Wizzy though, and she took a seat beside Nella after getting her food. Better that they not talk then.

Josh managed to down a little salad plus a grilled cheese sandwich. Would he wind up eating anything at the Joint later? He doubted it, no matter how things went.

He finished quickly, glad to leave the cafeteria before it appeared anyone else was heading out. He went straight to his apartment and changed clothes into a short-sleeved navy T-shirt and jeans. Casual things he would wear if he wasn't living here. Things he could now wear outside for whatever happened later.

He pulled out a denim jacket. It might be too warm outside for it, but it might also help hide any wiring if he was prepped to let the authorities hear what was going on around him.

Not time to go yet, but he figured it would be best to hang out here till he needed to meet up with Scott. But would Janna come first?

Could she hide enough to get here?

Sitting in the living room to wait, he soon heard a soft knock at his apartment door. He quickly opened it, then closed and locked it after Janna came in, looking up at him with quizzical and caring green eyes.

"Are you—" she began, but he drew her close and planted his lips on hers before she could finish.

He'd at least take advantage of her being here, of seeing her for what might be the final time. And did they ever make good use of being together for that short afternoon.

But all good things had to come to an end—hopefully not permanently. Eventually, Janna, nude and gorgeous and panting softly after their brief encounter, was the one to roll away from him on his bed.

"Oh, Nolan," she managed to say. "That was—that was so wonderful. But I'm getting concerned—"

"Yeah," he agreed. "It's nearly time for me to get ready."

She stood up, pulling a sheet around her so he no longer had a view of her luscious body. "Then you're going to go. I can't convince you otherwise."

He laughed slightly. "What do you think? Police Chief Sherm has promised I'm going to have a lot of people watching me."

"I get it. I just hope they can protect you." Janna moved close once more, gave him another kiss, then let go of the sheets but turned away. He got a great view of her back and behind as she started getting dressed. No time for either of them to shower now.

He grabbed his own clothes off the chair, then got dressed as well. Since they were at his apartment, he was the one to check the hallway for anyone in the hall. He told Janna it was empty and okay for her to leave.

He swallowed his sorrow as he shut the door behind her. Had that been their last time together?

Chapter 20

After cautiously leaving the apartment building—and, fortunately, not getting seen since this was another time when most staffers were out working with dogs—Janna spent a while at the shelter clinic checking on their patients, maybe even more than she needed to. But although she also brought Wizzy out for a short walk, she needed to use up more time before she had to leave.

She still hadn't asked Scott or Nella if she could hang out with them while Nolan went to the Joint. She would simply follow and watch, and only get involved if it seemed to make sense.

Simply? No, it was unlikely to be simple.

She didn't even know where they were supposed to meet whoever it was, other than how they'd told the stalker to come to Chance.

She was aware of the time, though. And so, just before three o'clock, she leashed Wizzy, and they left the clinic. As far as she knew, Kyle might still arrive there that afternoon, but she'd been in touch and let him know all was well. Maybe he'd come, or maybe he'd just rely on Nella or Scott to peek in and let him know if anything seemed wrong with one of their patients.

Not that the directors here would be around either, but Kyle didn't know that. And Janna felt fairly confident that their patients would be fine without further care today. Plus, a staffer or two would check on them and their water supplies, and give them dinner later.

Janna didn't think she'd be back that afternoon, unless Kyle contacted her about a problem. He was aware, though, of her likely unavailability even though he didn't know the real reason why.

That was her own stupidity. She shouldn't worry so much about Nolan and what was going on with him. He had real law enforcement people, trained to handle bad situations and experienced at it, watching out for him.

What could she, a vet tech who might not even know how to protect herself in a bad situation, do to help?

It didn't matter. She wanted to be there just to see if she might be of any kind of assistance.

She fastened Wizzy carefully in the back seat of her car, as she always did. Now, she waited in the parking lot, watching both Scott's and Nella's empty cars. Surely, they'd use one of them to take Nolan wherever he needed to go.

Scott did come through the security fence with Nolan a short while later and shooed him carefully into the front seat of his car, the special black SUV he used with a large hatch. Nella followed almost immediately and sat in the back seat. Then they drove off.

Janna had to be careful not to be too obvious, but she followed at a distance, though close enough that she could keep an eye on them. She could always say she had to go shopping or something if they saw her, rather than heading directly for the downtown clinic.

But if they did see her, they didn't stop. Instead, they headed into the heart of Chance's downtown, a few long blocks away.

There seemed to be a little less traffic than usual. Were people being told to stay away? Janna hadn't heard anything.

Soon, Scott parked in a downtown parking lot, not far from the civic center and a lot of stores and restaurants. Janna pulled into a different lot nearby. There seemed to be ample parking on the street, but the spaces all had meters. Janna didn't know how long she'd need to have her car there. A regular lot seemed better.

She put the ticket into her small purse and got Wizzy out of the back seat, then walked past some of the other cars that were entering and headed toward the street. She did see Scott, Nella and Nolan when they reached the sidewalk. Where were they headed?

And where was the usual crowd of people walking around downtown Chance? She hadn't seen any cops stopping people, and no one had stopped her.

Although could that have been because of who she happened to be tailing? Maybe anyone watching would have thought they were together, even though she had avoided getting too close.

She saw them stop outside the Joint Restaurant, then go inside.

The Joint. Was that where things were going to happen? Janna had eaten there often, lunch with fellow vet techs and dinners with friends or dates. Good food at affordable prices, a nice, friendly atmosphere. She had even been able to bring Wizzy with her, although she always had him lie down under the table.

Should she go in now? Heck, why not? She'd sometimes park in the restaurant's lot behind it and gone inside through the back door with Wizzy. She wasn't going to move her car now, but she might be less obvious if she nevertheless went in the back way.

She moved close to the restaurant with Wizzy and walked slowly around to the back. She kept watch but didn't see anyone at all at the moment—no cops and no strangers who might be the person who'd sent that threat to Nolan.

The back door was unlocked, but she opened it carefully. A buzz of voices crept out at her. The place did have customers, apparently, despite whatever was going on.

She walked in with Wizzy and looked around even more. There were wooden booths along the wall, with tables in the center. It was far from being as full as she'd sometimes seen it, but this wasn't a time of day likely to be crowded.

People were talking to one another, raising sandwiches or glasses or forks full of food to their mouths. An aroma of food filled the air as well, and servers in white shirts and dark trousers, both men and women, appeared to be talking to customers, maybe taking orders or bringing food to them.

She glanced at the wall toward the usual pictures of downtown Chance above the booths.

Yes, it appeared to be a normal restaurant afternoon, as far as she could tell.

One of the booths near the back door was empty. "Come, Wizzy," she said to her pup and they both headed there. "Down." Wizzy did as she said, lying down under the table.

A male server came over, looked first at Wizzy and then at Janna. "Are you with the group?" he asked.

The group? Was there supposed to be some kind of party here today? Or was this not-very-large bunch of people composed of undercover officers?

Whatever the situation, Janna didn't want to get booted out, and so she nodded. "That's right."

"But—"

As the guy spoke, Janna saw some people enter through the front door—the people she expected to see there that day, Scott, Nella...and Nolan. She nodded in their direction. "I'm with them."

"Got it." Then the server left.

But as tempted as Janna was to go join them, she stayed where she was as they sat down in a booth near that door. Until she figured out what was going on, it would be better for now just to observe.

While she watched, she noted that Nolan faced generally in her direction, but he seemed to be talking a lot to Scott and Nella. As far as she could tell, he hadn't noticed Wizzy or her. That was fine.

A different server came over, and Janna ordered a chicken salad sandwich and coffee. She checked the time. Three twenty now. Ten minutes till the mystery person was supposed to arrive, assuming they'd be on time.

A few minutes later, Scott and Nella rose and went to another table near Nolan's, but not right next to it.

Nolan moved into one of the seats they had occupied so he faced that door.

A server brought him a glass of water and a menu. And spoke with him briefly before leaving.

Janna wished she could join him. But she knew the better thing to do was to stay there.

And watch.

Okay, so now what? Nolan was here. But he'd no idea if the person threatening him was here as well.

He'd been told that most of the people who'd be at the restaurant that afternoon would be undercover cops sent there by the Chance PD, although some might be friends or others who knew what was going on and would leave as soon as anything seemed to happen.

He wasn't about to get up and look around to see if he recognized anyone.

But would his tormentor come over and talk? Grab him and try to pull him out of the restaurant? Kill him right here?

Enough of that. There was all sorts of protection around him. He just had to trust the authorities.

But as a writer who researched all sorts of bad things and wrote about some of the worst, he couldn't help worrying. Trusting no one. Not even himself.

A middle-aged female server came over—real, or someone undercover? It didn't matter since she'd brought a menu and now asked if he wanted anything. He ordered coffee to give him something more than water to drink while he waited.

But how long would that be? He glanced at his watch.

Three thirty.

Should he at least stand up to make it obvious where he was? He had to assume whoever it was knew what he looked like.

Too bad he didn't also know who it was. He'd sic the cops around here on them right away.

Yeah. Right.

The server brought his coffee over, plus some crackers. "Let me know if you want anything else, okay?"

Like getting out of here? Telling her that, whatever her real reason for being here, wasn't going to get him anywhere.

He considered digging the phone out of his pocket and trying to call again, ask when they'd get there.

But what good would that really do?

He took a sip of coffee, considered opening the cracker package and decided against it.

He definitely wasn't hungry.

He glanced again at his watch. One minute gone. Time was dragging. But still, whoever it was hadn't come here or contacted him. Maybe he should—

He swallowed his gasp as a woman slipped onto a chair across from him at the table. "Nolan? So glad to see you."

He knew her, though not well. He'd known her somewhat even before he started researching the restaurant story. It was Tanya Andershoot, wife of Declan, the surviving co-owner of Great Meals Restaurant in San Diego. Nolan had met all four in charge of the restaurant, including Jaxon's widow Luisa, when he used to visit Great Meals before any of this had begun. And he'd questioned the survivors when doing the research for his current novel.

"Good to see you too, Tanya."

The fortysomething woman's short black hair now had a few gray strands. She wore a long black skirt and short-sleeved black blouse, a similar outfit to what he had seen her in before. The purse she carried over her arm looked like a luxurious leather one, or was it fake? He doubted they made a whole lot of money running Great Meals.

The expression on her pixieish but slightly aging face was not similar to anything he'd seen before. Her light brown eyes were wide open and appeared horrified.

"What's wrong?" he asked. And why the heck was she here, so far from San Diego, especially at this time, when he was supposed to meet—

Her? But—

"Everything's so strange," she said with a soft wail. "Some guy called with a strange voice and said that I'd better come meet you here and bring you with me or my husband, Declan, will be killed today, like poor Jaxon was. I was so scared I just did what he said—including not calling the police."

Some guy. The same person who'd threatened Nolan now threatened Tanya that the remaining owner of Great Meals would be killed? It was a man, then?

That made some sense. But who was it?

And was anyone watching Nolan now? Some of the people here had to be undercover cops, considering what Sherm had worked out. Plus, Nolan was wearing a wire, so surely they were listening.

"I am sorry to hear that," he said, and he definitely was. "I'd really hate for anything to happen to Declan too. I came here to meet someone who made a similar threat but didn't identify themselves. I couldn't make it to San Diego because I was here researching—"

Okay. Enough. Too much information.

"What is it that you're supposed to do?" he finished.

"I guess the man was angry that you wouldn't meet him in San Diego. He told me to drive here and meet up with you and bring you back to Great Meals with me. Please, please come with me, Nolan. I don't know what I'd do if he hurt Declan because you didn't come with me."

What should he do? Even if the undercover cops around here stormed Tanya and took her into custody for further interrogation, what good would that do?

How could they protect Declan?

And so he said, loud enough that he undoubtedly could be heard over his wire, "Okay. I'll go with you. We need to be sure Declan stays unharmed."

The local cops should be able to follow Tanya's car, let the authorities in San Diego know what was happening and protect Declan there. Right?

And so Nolan stood, grabbed a few dollars out of his wallet that should cover the cost of the coffee, placed them on the table and walked out with Tanya.

"I'm parked in the lot behind this place," she said and motioned for him to follow her out of the building.

There were a few people standing around outside, but even if they did happen to be undercover officers no one approached, which was best.

Was he being foolish for listening to this woman? If this was one of his stories, there'd be something going on that wouldn't be obvious.

Had Tanya been the one who murdered Jaxon? That was how Nolan might handle it in one of his books, but that surely wasn't reality. Was it?

"So tell me," Tanya said as they headed around the building toward the parking lot. "I've read your book that was loosely based on what happened at Great Meals. The killer was one of the regular patrons. But our local cops said they'd done a lot of checking and interrogating people like that, as well as Declan and Luisa and me. And no one got arrested. So how did you plot your story?"

That seemed an odd thing for her to ask. And Tanya seemed to have calmed down. A lot.

"Well, I can tell you about it. But right now, before we get on the way, there's a phone call I need to make to—"

"The cops, I bet," Tanya suddenly hissed. She grabbed his arm and led him to a silver SUV parked in the lot, shoving him toward the passenger door.

"What's going on?" he asked her—as he saw her reach into that expensive-looking handbag of hers.

"We need to go to save Declan," she spat through her perfect teeth.

But Nolan had a bad feeling about this. A really bad feeling. "Did you set my house on fire? Shoot at me?" he had to ask.

"What are you talking about?" she demanded. "Why would you think that was me?"

But her words, her tone, seemed to imply she knew

what he was talking about, even though there'd been no publicity about it.

Riding with this apparently angry, maybe crazy woman made no sense. Not even to save another life.

And so Nolan just stood there, trying not to look around. Where were the people who were supposed to be his backup?

Chapter 21

Sitting at her table sipping some herbal tea, Janna had watched as a pretty middle-aged woman joined Nolan. Was she the stalker?

But Nolan seemed friendly with her as they talked, if Janna could tell from this distance. Did he know her?

The woman's face looked scared. But was that just an act?

Janna practically jumped to her feet when Nolan rose and walked out the door with her. Where were they going?

Why weren't the cops stopping them? She figured they'd have some kind of equipment on Nolan so they could hear what he was saying. Did they think he was okay?

Did they believe he'd be worse off if they stormed them?

Or was she just overthinking this?

Well, Janna might be just a vet tech, not a cop, and not one of the heroes of Nolan's books, but she could at least follow as a concerned, oblivious citizen. Right?

Not knowing how things would work out, she'd already given her server her credit card to swipe and told her to charge anything Janna ordered on it, even though she might not get a chance to see the bill. Kind of dumb, maybe, but it seemed more practical under these circumstances.

"Come, Wizzy," she told her dog. Janna stood and walked toward the front door, where Nolan and that woman had just left.

Some of the other people at the tables inside had risen too. Cops? Janna hurried to get out the door before they did. Okay, maybe this was dumb too. Maybe she should just rely on the cops, as Nolan seemed to be doing.

She'd just stay back and watch, to make sure nothing bad happened.

But if something looked wrong? Could she bring herself to interfere?

Maybe so, if it could help to make sure Nolan remained okay.

She and Wizzy turned the corner around the building to head for the parking lot behind the Joint, following Nolan and the woman. Janna glanced behind her. A few other people had left the restaurant after her, but none appeared to be following.

As she and Wizzy reached the parking lot, she did notice some other people hanging around there chatting. Were they paying attention to Nolan and that woman? Could she assume they were cops undercover, and they'd make sure he remained okay?

And if she did anything, would she simply be behaving stupidly?

She'd try to be careful. But if Nolan seemed in trouble—

He'd been hanging out near that silver SUV with the woman for a few minutes now. The passenger door was open, and Janna wondered if the woman was trying to get Nolan to go inside.

They both appeared stressed, and their voices seemed raised, even though she couldn't hear what they were saying. The woman had one hand in her purse, and Nolan kept looking down at it.

Janna's imagination—her wannabe writer's imagination—went wild.

Surely the woman wasn't carrying a gun. And wouldn't she have aimed it at Nolan if she was? Although with other people around...

Surely the woman wouldn't know some could be undercover cops. Or would she?

The woman pushed Nolan toward the seat, hard, yet he resisted and stood his ground outside the car.

Janna might be able to help him. Or rather, Wizzy could.

"Wizzy, run! Go see Josh!"

Her smart Australian shepherd mix looked at her, then toward Nolan and bolted in that direction.

Janna froze for a moment. Had she sent her beloved Wizzy into danger?

But when Nolan saw Wizzy coming, he knelt and held out his arms.

The woman appeared confused and upset and—yes, she drew a handgun out of her purse and aimed it at Nolan.

But in that instant, someone yelled "Drop it!" The people around the parking lot all drew guns and aimed them at the woman.

She looked furious. Shocked. Maybe even scared.

But she did obey as a couple of the guys pulled out badges and handcuffs.

And took her into custody.

"What were you doing there?" Nolan demanded a while later.

"I was worried about you," Janna replied.

He'd been taken separately to the police station by Scott. Apparently someone else had driven Janna and Wizzy there, and Nolan assumed she had also undergone interrogation while he was being questioned. Or at least the cops might have wanted to know what she'd been doing at the restaurant when they'd pretty well emptied it of civilians, and why she'd sent Wizzy in his direction.

So did Nolan, although he could guess. But he asked her anyway.

And though he didn't see Tanya, he assumed she was here someplace too, in custody, and also being questioned. In depth. Not only about why she'd confronted Nolan that way and tried to get him into her car, but also whether she had something to do with Jaxon Draybell's murder. Like having committed it. Could she have even threatened her own husband to get Nolan to do as she'd demanded, or at least tell people he was being threatened?

Now, Nolan was free to go, although he'd have to stay in touch as the investigation progressed.

With Tanya in custody, was the danger to him over? Could he go home and resume his real life?

Before he had much opportunity to ponder that, though, he'd seen Janna and Wizzy exit another room at the police station where she might have been questioned too. And now, in the hallway, he was conducting his own kind of interrogation of her.

"I think you know why I was there," she continued, gesturing for Wizzy to sit down by her side. Of course the good dog did.

A very good dog. Wizzy might have helped save Nolan from being shoved into that car, and—Janna looked into Nolan's face with her gorgeous green eyes.

"I could only guess what might happen today when you met whoever demanded that you show up to prevent someone else from being killed. My guess was that you would be the one in danger instead."

"I think you guessed right," he said, and took her into his arms. Hey, they weren't at the shelter. He could be himself, do what he wanted. And what he wanted was to give Janna a big kiss—which he did.

But he heard someone clearing his throat beside them, and Nolan stepped back.

Scott was there, grinning, and so was Nella at his side.

"Okay, you two," Scott said. "Try to keep things cool for now. Sherm wants us all in his office."

"I hope he's going to tell us what's going on and what they've learned from Tanya—assuming she's said anything at all."

"Let's go talk to Sherm." Scott turned and started down the hall toward Sherm's office, gesturing over his shoulder for them to follow.

Soon, Janna sat with Nolan, Scott and Nella facing Sherm across the desk.

Sherm appeared tired yet victorious, considering the way he smiled as he looked from one of them to the next.

"I assume you all want to hear what happened," he said, "or at least our take on it. We've been in touch with our San Diego PD cohorts, and they're still investigating there. And we're not done with it either."

"But do you know yet who's been threatening me?" Nolan asked, leaning toward the police chief. "Has it been Tanya all along? Or was she serious when she said someone else sent her here to get me so they wouldn't kill her husband?"

"All we can do so far is speculate," Sherm said, clasping his hands on his desk. "For one thing, I'm sure none of you will be surprised that Ms. Andershoot has lawyered up."

Nolan would definitely have been surprised if she hadn't. But that didn't confirm that she was guilty of anything but being smart in this situation.

"What she did say continuously was that she was ordered to come here by someone to get you, Nolan, to go back to San Diego with her, where that person would take over and talk to you—and in that case would not kill her husband. She indicated she was devastated by the fact that Jaxon Draybell had been murdered. That was the other guy who owned the restaurant, right?"

Nolan nodded. "Did she say who did that? Or did the San Diego police you spoke with let you know?"

"Ms. Andershoot said she had no idea. The cops? Well, they indicated Ms. Andershoot herself remained on the list of suspects—which sounded right to me. I couldn't get too detailed in our questioning, especially since she didn't have counsel present at the time. But my initial take on it? I think she was having an affair with the guy and wound up killing him herself. Oh, I gathered she felt bad—at least somewhat. And she didn't sound thrilled that she had to struggle to keep that restaurant going. The two wives apparently left most of the hard work and details to their husbands, but with Jaxon dead and Declan devastated by it, both women, including Luisa Draybell, had to do a lot more work than just overseeing the food preparation and service."

"And yet Tanya came all the way to Chance to confront me—under orders or not." Nolan shook his head. "It doesn't make a lot of sense."

Sherm laughed a bit grimly. "Well, murders don't, and neither do all efforts of the guilty to protect themselves." He leaned back and crossed his arms.

Nolan noted that those with him, including Janna, Scott and Nella, appeared confused. As was he.

Janna leaned over a bit and petted Wizzy before she spoke. "Let's assume for now that Tanya was the killer. Why wouldn't she just stay home and continue to act innocent and devastated at the loss of her husband? Why threaten Nolan?"

"Because I wrote a book about it," Nolan said. "I'm sure most murderers want to keep what they did away from public attention as much as possible. The local cops had apparently been stymied, which was one reason I used that murder as the basis for my story. That might have led to local authorities staying focused on it—which was what I'd hoped. But why threaten me this way now? The book was already out there."

"But you just recently did something to make it even

more public again," Janna said, sounding excited. Even Wizzy stood up and stared at her, wagging his tail.

"What was that?" Sherm asked.

"Oh, my publicist was upset that I was in hiding and couldn't get out there and do public appearances and signings," Nolan said. "Janna was kind enough to help me get a whole lot of signed stickers sent to booksellers to place inside my books and hopefully help to sell a lot more of them."

"And that upset the killer again." Sherm sounded excited. "Makes sense. We'll have to keep that in mind during our investigation of Tanya. And let the San Diego cops know, too. In fact, we'll need to extradite her there for further review and going to trial for murder, since it happened there."

"This should certainly be interesting," Nolan said.

"Material for another book." That was Janna, beside him.

"For me or for...someone else," he said, and they smiled at each other.

The meeting ended, with Sherm agreeing to keep all of them informed as to how things worked on his end, although he warned them that his ability to share much more was unlikely. "The two of you are likely to be witnesses if Tanya is brought to trial, and I can't taint any of the evidence by being too open about it with you."

Nolan wondered if he already had done so in this get-together, but he wasn't about to say anything.

He walked out with the others to the parking lot. Scott and Nella had driven there from the shelter. Nolan still didn't know who'd brought Janna here, but he gathered that her car remained parked near the Joint.

Scott offered to drive Wizzy and her there to get it, and Nolan joined them.

When they reached her car, Nolan got out too, wanting to spend more time with her for now. He couldn't be certain things were over. He had to keep playing his role as Josh for now, he supposed.

What if Tanya had been telling the truth, or some version of it, and she'd been sent to get him?

So for this evening, at least, and maybe longer, he would remain Josh.

He did manage to get Janna to visit him for a short while in his apartment just after dinner, before she returned to her own place in Chance.

And things remained somewhat normal, if being Josh at the shelter was normal, for the next week. But he did spend time working with Spike, which he always enjoyed. And he visited the shelter vet clinic when he could and enjoyed when Janna came outside with Wizzy for fun and training.

Plus, they got some apartment time in whenever possible. Secretly? He doubted it, but none of the other staff members gave him a hard time about it.

At least some of the time they were together there, they discussed her writing, including some new edits she showed him after getting his final comments on her full manuscript. She was good, and he hoped he was helping her get even better.

Hopefully, she'd have a publishable finished manuscript soon. He'd already promised he would let Bruce know she was sending it to him—after Nolan's guidance.

For now, he remained a staffer at the shelter. But for how long?

Then, one afternoon, Scott asked him to come to his office for a conversation with Sherm. Only it turned out to be a conference call. Janna was there for it too, along with Wizzy.

"I've got the San Diego prosecutor on the phone with us," Sherm said. "She has some information and a request for you."

It turned out not exactly to be a request. After all, they could have issued subpoenas to get Janna and him to go to San Diego.

Yes, Tanya had been indicted. They didn't get into what the evidence was against her, but she would stand trial, though not until the usual sixty days in California had passed.

Nolan did ask some questions. No, there were no more guarantees here than in other cases. But he gathered they were pretty damn sure they had their murderer in custody.

"Sounds good," Scott said after they hung up.

"Yes, it does," Janna said. She looked at Nolan. "We should plan to travel to San Diego together in a few weeks."

Was that a touch of sorrow in those amazing green eyes? Surely not.

"I'll look forward to that for many reasons," Nolan told her.

They had dinner together again in the cafeteria that

evening. And yes, they sneaked separately up to his apartment and had some wonderful alone time there—well, alone with Wizzy on the floor near them.

But Nolan knew it was time. He needed to talk to Janna.

And so, before she left for the night, he asked her to sit down with him in the living room.

"You won't be surprised," he said, "to learn that I'm about ready to stop living here at the shelter. I've received no more threats since Tanya was arrested, and my agent and publicist also haven't heard anything more. I'm really happy we've been able to spend more time together, and going to San Diego together soon should be enjoyable in many ways, but—"

"But I was waiting for you to make that decision," Janna said. "If all goes as we anticipate, you'll now be Nolan forever again. And not here."

They kissed warmly before she left for the night. Nolan appreciated her understanding. And they'd still have at least a few more days like this before he figured out where he'd be living next and took off.

But damn, he was going to miss this wonderful woman.

Only—well, he had an idea.

He needed to figure it out. Contact his people. Leave the shelter, at least for a while. He'd confirm things with Scott or Nella, but figured they'd be okay with it.

With luck, he'd soon be getting his real life back.

Chapter 22

Janna had just finished her shift at the downtown clinic. She was happy to be heading to the shelter, as always. And hopefully engaging in what had become the routine there, including—delightfully—time with Nolan.

At least he was still there. For now. But it was clear that he intended to leave soon, maybe forever.

Their trip to San Diego was scheduled for just three days from now. At least they'd get to spend even more time together then—but for how long? Probably not more than a couple of days. She wasn't sure what the trial schedule was, but neither one should have to testify for very long.

She'd gotten her credit card back immediately at the restaurant, so she'd be able to use it to charge her expenses on the trip. And no, she'd checked and the server she'd trusted with it hadn't charged anything.

"Okay, Wizzy," she said to her wonderful dog as she got him from his clinic enclosure. "Let's go to the shelter."

"Hey, Janna," Kyle called to her from his office as she walked by. "There's someone here to see you."

She headed to his office and looked in—and was shocked to see Nolan.

"What are you doing here?" she demanded. "Away from the shelter?"

"I wanted to talk to you away from there," he said, coming toward her. He turned back to Kyle. "Thanks for letting me in."

When he walked outside, of course Janna and Wizzy followed.

"Nolan, I don't…" Janna began as they stepped outside the clinic and onto the sidewalk.

"I won't know for certain until after the San Diego trial next week whether I'm leaving the shelter forever," he told her after giving her a brief kiss, maybe to shut her up. "But I have an idea. I've been thinking about it for days now, probably longer. And I've checked with my people about whether there's anyplace writer-me needs to live to continue my success, like back in San Diego."

"I assume we'll at least visit it next week, so you can decide," Janna said.

"I might put my place there on the market. I have some bad memories about San Diego, after all." They'd reached a corner, and Nolan stopped, looking down at Janna. "Now, I know this is a bit presumptuous of me, but I've been thinking about staying in Chance. I like this place, and in case I need to get back in the shelter, hanging around here—"

She got it. He didn't have to continue. "My condo's just a few blocks away. Let me show it to you, and if it looks okay for you to continue your writing…"

"I'll move in there, if that's all right with Wizzy and you." He bent down and patted her dog on the head.

Wizzy sat there looking up at him and wagged his tail.

"Oh, I think he'll be quite happy with you there with us." Janna was thrilled! She would actually be living with the renowned author Nolan Hoffsler.

The author—the man—she loved!

"And we can work together more on your writing," he continued. "I'll introduce you to my agent in person, not just on the phone. He's already expressed some interest in seeing your work, maybe because of how much I like it."

She laughed. "And advised me on it."

"Well, a little." She was about to object and thank him again for all his help, but he added, "Oh, and though I'll be writing here in Chance, there's no way I'll ever mention the Chance Animal Shelter in my writing."

"I figured." She threw her arms around him, careful to hang on to Wizzy's leash. Was anyone watching?

Who cared?

Nolan's head came down to hers, and their kiss was long and hot. "I love you, Janna," he said softly against her mouth.

"And I love you, Nolan. Now come on. Let me show you the place where you'll be living with me—for forever."

"Sounds good. Excellent, in fact. Oh, and maybe one of these days we can write a novel together," he said. "A romance with suspense, sure, but also a happily-ever-after."

"Based on ours," she said, and kissed him again.

* * * * *

HARLEQUIN
Reader Service

Enjoyed your book?

Try the perfect subscription for Romance readers and get more great books like this delivered right to your door.

See why over 10+ million readers have tried Harlequin Reader Service.

Start with a Free Welcome Collection with free books and a gift—valued over $20.

Choose any series in print or ebook.
See website for details and order today:

TryReaderService.com/subscriptions

RSBPA24R